My Neighbor is a Wolf

Delaine Walsh

For my mom who can never have too much spice.

For my readers who want care scenes and knotting, here you go.

CONTENT WARNING

Dear Reader,

Because it's me, this novella took a little morally gray turn that I wasn't anticipating. Below is a list of content warnings that some readers may find potentially triggering. Please do not hesitate to reach out if you have any questions!

- Physical assault, not between MCs

- Gun violence, not between MCs

- Bondage

- Breath play

- Knotting

- Pinch of primal chase with breeding

- Consensual and non-consensual biting

- Mentions of stalking, not between MCs

Happy Reading!
Delaine

CHAPTER ONE
Hunter

Thursday Night

Double checking I had everything I needed, I set the last bag of supplies by my front door. I went over the list in my mind while staring at the bags in front of me. The last few hours had been spent gathering the last minute things from around my apartment.

The full moon was in two days and, man, was I feeling it. My mind was always a bit chaotic leading up to my monthly hunting trip and a decent eight hours of sleep had evaded me these last few days.

Turning from the pile, I made my way to my weight bench in the corner of my living room. It wasn't a fancy set up by any means, but it did the job. Even after spending the last few hours packing, I knew I wouldn't be able to go to sleep right then. I needed to distract myself.

Several sets later, my muscles were aching. I sat on the floor and prepared for my post-workout meditation. It was a good way to clear my mind, especially when I was chomping at the bit from not shifting for a few weeks.

Just as I closed my eyes, someone clambered up the steps. *Shitty apartment layouts.* There were four apartments on this floor. While my unit had the largest square footage, I had to deal with it being next to the stairs.

I did my best to continue, forcing myself to focus on my breathing once more, but heavy footsteps caused my ceiling to creak. These thin walls and floors were notorious for letting every sound through.

There was no way I was finishing. Running my hands through my hair, I opened my eyes and glanced at the clock behind me to check the time.

2 a.m.

That checked out. Rachael, my upstairs neighbor, had a boyfriend who would come by her place around this time. I have never had a full conversation with Rachael. She introduced herself in passing a few days after she moved in. Everything else I simply learned from living under her, including that asshole's name.

Chad. The unemployed alcoholic who didn't deserve to breathe the same air as her. She screamed at him enough times about getting sober and finding a job for me to remember it. Just the thought of him near her made my blood boil with hatred.

By the sound of it, he was coming home drunk even now and would be attempting to wake up his girlfriend for a quickie. She would usually comply, but lately, she had welcomed his advances less and less. So much so that I hadn't heard the bastard stumbling through the building in over a week.

I had probably missed my opportunity to ask her out. When our paths crossed while doing laundry, I was never able to keep my eyes off of her. She was everything I had come to love about human women and more. Rachael was beautiful, with curves that she constantly tried to hide under oversized clothing and long legs that I craved to have wrapped around my shoulders. Her red hair was always pulled back in a bun on the top of her head, with loose, wavy strands falling around her face. I wanted nothing more than to feel their softness between my fingers.

But apparently, she still had a boyfriend. A shitty one, but a boyfriend nonetheless.

I stood up and made my way to the kitchen for a bottle of water, pushing the thoughts of her down into the recesses of my mind. We were not compatible, and the sooner I came to terms with that, the better.

I pressed the bottle to my lips and focused on listening for the typical series of events that I had come to expect. A slammed door. A couple knocks. Several more loud footsteps. A loud thump. Then snoring.

A door slammed right on cue.

But the knocks didn't follow. Instead, what sounded like the same door being thrown open and hitting something rattled the walls. Shouting filled the air, then silence.

That was when I smelled it. Blood.

What the fuck?

Maybe something had fallen and broken. *But I hadn't heard anything remotely close to that.*

I should have left it alone, but something pushed me to leave the comfort of my own apartment and climb the stairs to the second floor. Chad's words were loud enough to be heard as I stood outside the door, my fist poised to knock.

"You don't get to tell me no tonight!"

Rage coursed through my body. My fist fell to my side, shaking with fury. Without thinking, I kicked down the door and headed straight to the bedroom. Chad had Rachael by the throat, shoved against the wall.

Her eyes were wide with terror. That was not the look of someone who was participating consensually. Blood dripped from a split in her lip. She clawed at the fingers wrapped around her neck as Chad's free hand forced its way under the oversized shirt Rachael was wearing.

"Get your fucking hands off of her," I seethed. His hand under her shirt froze as he turned to look at me.

"How the hell did you get in here?" His hands dropped to his sides. Rachael crumpled to the floor and gasped for breath as Chad charged at me. Bone crunched under my fist as it made contact with his jaw.

He collapsed to his knees, and as he tried to stand I towered over him. "Leave. Now."

"The hell I will!" He spit blood near my feet and mine boiled with rage. It took everything in me not to shift and tear this shitty excuse of a man apart limb from limb.

My hand wrapped around the collar of his shirt and dragged his ass out the apartment door. He kicked and attempted to tear himself from my grip until we were standing on the sidewalk. I released my hold, letting him fall in a mess of limbs. Before he could stand, I pressed my foot into his chest and pinned him to the ground.

"Don't. Come. Back." My words came out as a growl, punctured each time by my foot pressing down a fraction into him. His fingers clawed at my ankle as his eyes went big and his face turned red from the inability to draw in enough air.

He was getting a taste of his own torture and I couldn't help but smirk down at him. This asshole had hurt her. That look on her face when I stepped into her apartment will forever be burned into my mind.

When I finally stepped away, I remembered Rachael was still upstairs and I needed to check on her. Without looking back, I rushed back to her apartment. The front door barely hung on its hinges and

I made a mental note to offer to fix that. At first glance, it looked like she had left. I stepped into the living room and peered in to see if she was still in the bedroom. I didn't want to scare her.

That's when something hard hit the back of my skull. Stars swirled in my vision. My knees buckled from underneath me, and I landed on the carpet on all fours as my ears rang.

My body was going into fight or flight mode. No matter what it chose, it wanted to shift and I wasn't going to be able to stop it.

Shit. This was not good.

Chapter Two
Rachael

I should have been running. At the very least, screaming for help. But no. My dumbass was staring at the *wolf* in the middle of my living room.

I closed my eyes and willed it away. Obviously, this was a concussion-induced hallucination. There was no way this was real.

But when my eyes blinked open, it was still there. The wolf stared back at me, its gold eyes bright enough that they nearly glowed gold. They reminded me of Hunter's, the man who just saved me from my ex. The man who had to live somewhere in this building because I always saw him in the laundry room downstairs in a hallway that seemed like it should lead somewhere, but didn't.

The man I always felt watching me after that day I introduced myself, but who never spoke to me again. Because who would be interested in a woman with thick thighs and a large belly? Definitely not a man who obviously had a six pack and whose biceps were as big as my head. He was built like a fucking tree, one I wanted to wrap my legs around and cling to like a koala.

A low growl snapped me out of my fantasy. *Fucking idiot.* There was a wolf standing feet from me and here I was daydreaming about mounting my neighbor.

The creature took a step towards me, baring its teeth in an angry snarl that had me gripping the bat in my hand a little tighter. It took another step and the breath caught in my lungs. I should have run, screamed, anything. Instead, when it was close enough that I could feel its warm exhale on my legs, I swung.

My bat made contact with something and the wolf went from advancing to lying on the floor. It was still, its fur as dark as the sky at midnight shining in the light cast from the small lamp on the end table.

"Shit," I muttered, dropping the bat at my feet. *Was it dead?* "Shit, shit, shit." I rushed forward checking for some sign of life. The rising and falling of its chest confirmed it wasn't dead.

I plopped down on the floor as I exhaled, releasing some of the tension that had built in my chest. The hardwood was cold on my legs and I realized I never put on pants after Hunter dragged Chad out of here. I had been too worried about Hunter losing the fight and Chad coming back to finish what he started.

There was no doubt in my mind that Chad would come back. I still couldn't believe my ex broke into my apartment and tried to force himself on me.

Maybe I should call the police. The thought made sense but as my eyes landed on the unconscious animal still laying on my floor. *Maybe animal control?*

I realized none of that was not an option. What would I have even said? *There's an unconscious wolf in my living room because I hit it over the head with my baseball bat.* There was just no way anyone would believe me. I pressed the palms of my hands into my eyes until I saw spots.

My throat tightened and the back of my eyes burned with the need to cry while I tried to figure out where I royally fucked up. I had kicked

Chad out after the last time he came home drunk and got a little too rough for my liking. It was a consent thing and he was not doing it for my pleasure. His nasty hands were doing things I didn't like and, when I told him to stop, he didn't listen. So I kneed him in the junk and he waddled out of my place, my door nearly hitting his ass as I slammed it behind him.

Thankfully, I was in between clients at work and the next big project wasn't starting for a few weeks so my boss was okay with me taking some time off. The space to clear my head and figure out what I wanted my next move to be was helpful. If I saved up for a few months, I could move to a new place.

Something called me to stay here though. It may have only been a few months, but I loved living in this small town. Maplewood Hollow had it all, from a little antiquities shop to a diner. Not to mention the cute guy from the laundry room—the same guy who came to my rescue tonight. Then in a blink of an eye, a wolf stood in his place.

A WOLF?

A laugh escaped my lungs because I knew how crazy my thoughts sounded. I mean, I believed in the supernatural stuff like witches and ghosts. The normal things. This town was known for attracting some weird stuff. But people who could turn into animals? There was no way Hunter was a wolf. *Right?*

A groan pulled me from my thoughts and I knew the universe was playing a cruel joke on me because it sounded human. I dropped my hands and froze when my focus landed on Hunter as he sat up, rubbing the back of his head and blinking.

His brows pinched together in confusion while he looked around my living room as if trying to understand where he was. When his gaze landed on me, his features relaxed for a split second before his eyes widened. He turned his body toward me and moved to stand.

"Rachael, I..." His words trailed off when I scrambled away from him. My legs failed me as I attempted to rise and put space between us. Instead, I not so gracefully backed into the end table, sending the only source of light in the room crashing to the floor. As soon as the ceramic base hit the wood, it shattered and plunged my apartment into darkness.

"Shit," I muttered. Feeling for the edge of the end table, I used it to pull myself up so I could go in search of the light switch in the kitchen.

"Rachael, don't try to walk around. You're going to step on—" His words were cut off by my scream as I stepped directly onto a broken piece of lamp. Pain sliced through the underside of my foot while a string of expletives left my mouth. My nails dug into the wooden top of the table I was still holding onto, trying not to fall over as a shooting sensation spread through my lower leg.

"Don't move," Hunter said. I could barely hear his words over the pounding of my heart in my ears. Rustling sounds were followed by the kitchen light being turned on. Hunter began rummaging around my kitchen drawers like he was searching for something.

Tears clouded my vision as I looked down at my right foot. A piece of thin ceramic, slightly bigger than a quarter, stuck out from my heel. There was a throbbing ache that radiated from the wound, made worse the longer I stared at it. I leaned onto the small table and settled my foot on my left knee. Without thinking, I pulled out the offending shard.

Blood flowed from the wound in a steady stream. Time slowed as I watched it leave a thin line of scarlet down my leg until it pooled on the floor.

"Fuck," Hunter shouted. Or at least I think he did. I lifted my head in time to see him close the distance between us in several large strides. "Why in the hell did you do that?" He pressed one of my kitchen towels to the wound, causing a hiss to escape from my clenched teeth. I remained perched against the end table while he worked to tightly wrap the towel around my foot.

Trying to find a way to distract myself from the dagger-like pain that was radiating from my foot, my eyes followed a path of ink that started at Hunter's forearm. It wrapped around his bicep and led to an intricate piece that connected his shoulder and arm. The tattoos stopped there, but a patch of the same dark hair that was on top of his head lined his chest. My hand flexed as I stopped myself from reaching out to run my fingers through it.

The hair continued down in a dusting along this man's well defined ab muscles until it disapp– *Wait, it didn't disappear.*

Hunter straightened himself at that exact moment and offered me his hand, but I was frozen, my gaze locked on his giant cock. *Did this man not realize he was standing in front of me like the statue of David?*

"You should probably sit down."

I still couldn't move, perched against the end table. My eyes found his face once again. Our gazes met and my knees threatened to give out as I stared into those bright brown eyes of his. I would let this man do anything he wanted to me.

What the hell is happening to me? I gave myself a mental chastising for thinking about sex right now. It was the blood loss. Because that's the only reason I would be having these thoughts after the shit show that just took place.

"You should go," I muttered, setting down my foot and doing my best to balance on my toes. Pain like a bolt of electricity shot through my leg. Tears pooled in the corners of my eyes but I blinked them away. I ignored his outstretched hand as I sidestepped him and hobbled towards the kitchen.

"Rachael, let me help you. You need stitches. And that towel definitely isn't sanitary." The floor creaked under his steps as he spoke, and within seconds, warm fingers wrapped around my upper arm. I froze, certain that if I turned around I'd give into whatever carnal desires were coursing through me right now.

Hunter took my silence as me needing further encouragement. "Please. I'll explain everything. I promise I'm not going to hurt you."

Why did he assume I thought he was going to hurt me? He was the one who had rescued me like a knight in shining armor from my asshole ex.

Then I remembered the whole wolf thing.

He thought...

I spun my body around as I yelled, "Hunter, it's because you're naked!" Instantly, I regretted the action. My head began swimming and my vision tunneled. I swayed where I stood, reaching out for something, anything, to help steady myself.

"Rachael?" Hunter sounded far away. The last thing I remembered before I slipped into the darkness was the sudden warmth surrounding me as my body was cradled against something hard.

Chapter Three
Hunter

Friday Morning

I hesitated on bringing Rachael to my apartment. It meant carrying her through the magical barrier into the section of the building for the *non-human* tenants. If she didn't accept us, this could be bad news. But my apartment was clean and I needed new clothes. Plus, there was nothing that a hospital would do that couldn't be done here and better. I needed to know she would be okay and something told me that I could trust her.

Liliana, a vampire and doctor, had just gotten home from her overnight shift at the hospital when she heard the commotion from next door. It had not been easy trying to get Rachael into my apartment. She quickly stitched her up, only needing to put in a couple, then called one of our other neighbors, Benny.

He was a kitchen witch who specialized in medicinal properties. There was a pot of tea brewing that should help with the pain and fight off any infections on top of speeding up healing. Between Liliana's expert care and Benny's magical brewing, I had a feeling Rachael would be okay. Though she would probably still have to stay off her feet for a few days, at least she wouldn't be miserable.

The door to my bedroom creaked as I peeked inside to check on her. She slept peacefully on my bed, my black sheets draped across her body. I had washed the dried blood off her as best I could without being too invasive before slipping a pair of my sweatpants over her bare legs. My apartment was typically kept colder to compensate for my higher core temperature and I didn't want her to be uncomfortable.

Satisfied she was still okay, I gently shut the door behind me and returned to my neighbors sitting at my small kitchen island. I had put on a pair of shorts while Liliana was caring for Rachael. Though they had seen it all before, now wasn't the time to be walking around my place like I lived in a nudist colony.

"Still sleeping?" Liliana asked while tracking my movements across the top of her mug.

"Yeah." I picked up my own mug full of coffee as I answered, then chugged half of its lukewarm contents to try and stifle the impending exhaustion overtaking my body. The sun was beginning to rise and usually I was already passed out for the day.

I scrubbed my face with my hands, scratching the hairs of my beard in thought. Rachael's door was still busted up. I had gotten it closed earlier but if anyone looked too closely, it wouldn't look good.

"Hey Benny, can you do me a favor? Will you see about getting Rachael's door fixed? You've got more contacts in this town and I don't want anyone thinking the worst and calling the cops."

"Sure thing."

"Oh, maybe change the locks, too?"

"Consider it done. You still planning on leaving for your hunting trip tomorrow?"

"Maybe," I answered, having forgotten about it until that moment. *Would I still go?* The full moon was on Saturday and if I didn't hunt...

"Well what about my dinner party on Sunday? I think Theo and Azalea are going to be back from their trip and are planning on coming! I'm so excited to start celebrating the holidays."

"I don't know," I mumbled.

I had never actually planned on going in the first place. Parties were definitely not my thing, even if I knew everyone. Though it would be nice to see Theo. He was a dragon shifter who lived in the fourth apartment and, up until last month, kept to himself. For as long as I lived here, he never ventured out unless hidden in the shadows. He wasn't very trusting, being the last of his kind. It had been nice finally meeting him when Azalea helped him feel more comfortable among the humans.

Azalea was a coven witch who owned an antiquities shop in town. Us paranormal beings knew that her store was filled with all sorts of magical things. Our short conversations always elated me, even if I barely understood what she was talking about half the time.

Contemplating if I should just bite the bullet and go, I downed the rest of my coffee and walked to the pot to pour another cup.

"Dude, you look like Liliana after she's done a twenty-four hour shift at the hospital," Benny said. He probably wasn't wrong. I needed a shower and sleep but I couldn't do that until I knew Rachael wasn't going to try and run as soon as she woke up.

"And what's that supposed to mean?" Liliana glared at him.

"It means he looks like a vampire who has been out in the sun all day. Come on Lil, keep up." Benny was the only one to laugh at his poor attempt at a joke.

"You're a fucking dumbass, Benny." Liliana rolled her eyes as he stopped laughing. These two bickered like siblings and most days I had to play peace negotiator so they could be in the same room together. I cleared my throat, effectively silencing the both of them.

"I don't want to go to bed until I know she's okay," I said. "And that she isn't going to try to leave right away." Benny and Liliana nodded. They were probably thinking I didn't want Rachael to go blabbing about us. While that was true, I was less concerned with that aspect. Humans needed a magical escort to enter past the barrier, though they were free to exit through it on their own. There was no way for them to simply stumble upon our retreat from the outside world.

Plus, who would believe her anyway? Sure, maybe a few would be suspicious, but without proof, there was no way for her to get people on her side. An apartment of supernatural beings living under everyone's noses. Even I barely thought it was possible.

No, the reason I wanted her around was because the wolf in me had laid claim to her. I needed her to stay. To pin her down to my bed and make her squirm under my touch. To trace my tongue along every sensitive area on her body and see what she tasted like. To feel the way she squeezed me as I knotted inside of her and had her screaming my name. To—

"Earth to Hunter." Liliana snapped her fingers in front of my face before throwing a thumb over her shoulder. "We've got company."

My eyes followed to where she was pointing and sure enough, Rachael was leaning against the doorframe. Her bandaged foot was propped up on her toes and a sweat coated her forehead.

I rushed to her, stopping short when I noticed her body tense.

"Hey," I whispered. "Are you okay?" *Of course she isn't okay and I am definitely not helping the situation by making it even more awkward with my dumbass questions.*

"Yeah. Well I mean..." She lifted her foot in response. Then she smiled and my chest tightened. It wasn't the one that made the corner of her eyes crinkle. Gods, I would give anything to see that smile more often. No, this smile was sad and more forced, like she was trying to not only convince me, but herself.

Her cheeks reddened when she met my eyes. I resisted the urge to reach out and run my thumb along the blushed skin. I knew I had to look like a lovesick teenager right now. She cleared her throat, not that she needed my attention. She already had it completely. "But I um, I really need to pee."

"Yeah, of course. Can I help?" I offered her my hand and hoped she would take it. She looked down at it, hesitating, then placed her palm in mine. Her fingers were soft and chilled against my own calloused and hot skin. She took a step, tumbling slightly when she put weight on her injured foot. Both of her hands clamped down on my forearms. I turned my own hands to gently grasp her arms and keep her steady.

"We'll just be going," Liliana called to us. Rachael peeked around me but I kept my back to them, offering nothing more than a grunt as the soft click of the front door let me know of their departure.

My apartment fell silent, the only sounds being the noise of the town outside the windows. Even those faded away when Rachael returned her gaze to me. Never had I occupied space so close to her before. If I had, I wouldn't have been able to stop the wolf inside me from claiming her. It was taking every ounce of control I had to not take her right then.

Her scent was intoxicating and I took a deep breath to solidify it in my mind. I wanted to remember it long after she left.

Rachael tried to take another step, her nails biting into my skin as her face scrunched. A hiss left her lips and I knew she was trying to hide how much pain she was really in. I didn't think before I scooped her up into my arms, not dwelling too long on how she immediately wrapped her arms around my neck.

"Hunter, I don't–" she started, but I cut her off.

"Let's cut it out with the fake protesting cause we both know you're fine with this. You're in pain and there's no need for you to be walking around."

She huffed in response, like a toddler who had just been told no to dessert before dinner. A smile spread across my lips as she settled against my chest without further complaint.

I walked us to the bathroom, flipping on the light with the hand under her legs. The four bulbs over the mirror filled the space in a luminescent glow. It wasn't anything too fancy but there was a separate shower stall and bathtub, which was a nice feature. Because there were less apartments on this floor, the floor plans were bigger. It was a huge selling point for me so I had more room when I shifted. I didn't feel the need to go camping in the woods for a weekend outside of my hunting trip just to let my fur hang loose.

I made my way over to the toilet, setting Rachael on her feet as gently as possible in front of it. She swayed slightly and I held onto her waist. Her body was inches away from mine, close enough that I felt her little huff of air across my bare chest. I looked down, meeting her narrowed eyes.

"What?" I asked, unsure what she wanted. She looked adorable like this but I had better sense than to tell a woman she looked cute when she was mad.

"Can I have some privacy?" Her eyes darted from my outstretched arms and back up.

"No." Rachael tried to interrupt but I pressed on. "I have zero faith in your ability to do this on your own. Just a few minutes ago, you couldn't even take a step without stumbling."

Her lips formed a tight line. She was trying to come up with a rebuttal but was having a hard time. We both knew I was right. This had turned into a game of who was going to give in first. The problem was I never backed down from a challenge.

"Fine," she muttered. I reached around her and lifted up the toilet seat cover while she shoved the sweatpants down from her hips. They pooled at her feet but her oversized shirt offered her privacy as I helped her sit down. When I was certain she wouldn't fall over, I released my hold on her waist and stepped back until I hit the bathroom vanity. But my eyes never left hers.

Everything about this woman called to me in a way that it hadn't before today. Being in her presence, touching her and talking with her, was a totally different ball game compared to our limited interactions in passing. I wanted more. My soul craved it. Even though I knew there was a chance she would leave my apartment screaming the first chance she got.

She cleared her throat, annoyance dripping from her tense posture and brows furrowing at my looming presence. Once again, we were engaged in a staring contest to see who would break. I could have left now that she was sitting, but there was a part of me that found this back and forth we had started very entertaining. I crossed my arms across my bare chest, casually leaning against the faux marble counter. A smile tugged at the corner of my lips.

"You could, at the very least, turn around." She rolled her eyes as she spoke.

"I could, but where would the fun be in that?"

"Hunter," she warned and I heard the threat in her voice. *Why was I playing a game with a woman who held my life in her hands?* Okay, so that may be a bit dramatic but I was still taking a risk. Playing nice would get me a lot further, even if it wasn't as much fun.

I turned my back to her, casually leaning on my hip against the faux marble counter. Out of the corner of my eye, I could see Rachael in the mirror. She was fiddling with the hem of her shirt with her injured foot stretched out in front of her. I could just make out some dried blood on the inside part of her other leg.

"I'm guessing this is your place?" she asked, her knee now bouncing anxiously.

"Yeah, I was worried about you. I didn't want to take you to the hospital and them ask a bunch of questions. Plus, a friend of mine is a doctor anyway so she did your stitches. And your place is still a mess from everything. Plus your door..." I trailed off. Oversharing was a nervous habit of mine.

Most people would have interrupted me but when I looked at Rachael she had a smile on her face. When I caught her gaze, she looked down at her hands, fiddling with the waistband of my sweats.

"Thank you. For last night." Her voice was small and I almost missed her words.

"You don't have to thank me."

"I do. If it weren't for you..." She stopped and looked up at me. A single tear fell from her eye. I gave her a slight nod, trying to express without words that it was okay. Her attention returned to her hands and that was the end of that conversation.

"Which apartment number is this? I didn't think any of them were this big. Plus, I've never seen you coming and going from any. Just always in the laundry room."

Leaving her question unanswered, I grabbed a clean washcloth from under the sink then walked over to the bathtub and turned on the water. Yes, I was avoiding answering her question. I lathered it up with some of my body wash and when I turned around, Rachael was finishing her business. Her smile was long gone.

"Here," I said, offering her the washcloth. She took it from me, her brow raised as she looked between the rag and me. "You have some dried blood left on your leg. I had tried to get up as much of it as I could earlier without being creepy." I pointed to the spot I was talking about.

"Oh," she whispered. She scrubbed at the spot and the blood disappeared as she did. I watched her face as she worked, her eyes growing sad and her skin paling slightly. A pang of guilt squeezed my heart and I chastised myself for being a jackass. She would have already been resting again if I had just helped her to the bathroom in peace.

Something in the air shifted. An awkwardness fell over us from my silent refusal to answer her question and I no longer knew what to do or say. I knew I needed to tell her everything but I thought I would have more time. At least until after she had healed. Rachael finished quickly, handing me back the cloth where I tossed it on the edge of the tub. I would deal with it later.

"Alright, sweetheart." I stepped in front of her, pushing my luck by placing my hands on her waist without permission. "Time to get you back to bed." She stood up, bringing the sweatpants up with her as she did. I picked her up and carried her back to the bedroom, hoping her lack of protest meant she was starting to trust me. When we made it to the bed, I helped her get settled and pulled the blankets over her legs.

"Let me know if you need anything. I'll just be out in the living room." I turned to leave, fighting the urge to stay when her words made me stop. Even if she did trust me, there was no guarantee I would be able to control myself. The object of my desire was in my bed and it wasn't easy denying my wolf what it wanted.

"I'm sorry." Her voice was so quiet and filled with pain. My chest tightened. *How could this woman believe for even one second that she did something wrong?* I spun on my heel, facing her as a stray tear slid down her cheek. She hastily wiped it away and looked down at her hands in her lap.

"Why the hell are you sorry?" I knelt down next to the bed, taking her chin between my thumb and finger. I urged her to look at me and unshed tears shined in the corners of her eyes. "I'm the one who broke into your apartment, essentially trashing it, and turned into a…" I paused, catching myself before I said too much and actually scared her off.

"A wolf?"

I looked up, surprised at her words, but even more surprised to see her completely calm.

CHAPTER FOUR
Rachael

Hunter blinked up at me, still kneeling on the floor next to the bed. At least this time he had on shorts. I couldn't judge the man if he walked around his own place naked. After all, I was the one intruding.

Unidentifiable sounds came from Hunter. His mouth opened and closed several times. "What?" he stammered.

"I mean, aren't you? A wolf? Or a werewolf I guess. Right?" I picked at my nails, avoiding the cuticles so I wouldn't bleed all over the poor man's bed. He had already done enough for me.

I met his eyes once more. They were still wide and his lips were pinched together. I had no idea why I was still here. It was obvious this man felt some sort of obligation to take care of me but that simply wasn't the case. Everything that happened last night was my fault. Chad wasn't a good person and I should have made sure he gave me back my key.

The back of my throat burned. I was thirsty and needed to cry which was never a good combination. I pushed the cover off my legs and swung them around until my feet hit the ground. As I attempted to push myself off the bed, Hunter stood to his full height and blocked my path.

"What are you doing?" he asked.

"I should go." I pulled myself up, my foot screaming in pain when I put weight on it. I did my best to ignore it by trying to take a step, but it was useless. My foot couldn't support my weight and I fell forward, straight into Hunter's naked chest.

He didn't miss a beat. His hands grabbed my hips and steadied me. I gave in, pressing my palms and forehead into the warm skin in front of me. The hair beneath my fingers was thick but soft.

"Rachael..." My name on his lips sent a shiver down my spine. It was filled with so much emotion. I tilted my head back, needing to see Hunter's face at that moment. He stooped down, our noses brushing together. The softness in his eyes made my heart skip a beat. Our lips were inches from each other and every nerve in my body demanded to know what it felt like to be kissed by him.

But the spell was broken when he lowered me back to the bed. "Rachael, please. I know you must be scared but I just need you to listen."

"Hunter, I'm not–" I tried to interrupt but it was like he couldn't hear me. His hands grabbed mine, squeezing them gently.

"Yes, I'm a wolf. But not a werewolf. I'm a shifter. I have control over when I do it. Well, ninety-nine percent of the time. High stress situations tend to trigger my fight or flight response, which is why it happened after you hit me with the baseball bat."

Well that made sense. Mostly.

"Oh, I'm s–"

"No, don't apologize. Seriously. I was this stranger who came into your apartment and you had every right. I'm the one who should be sorry. I mean, I am sorry. I broke into your place. It's my fault you hurt yourself. Not to mention I practically kidnapped you. And now I've put you in this tough spot."

Hunter kept talking, saying more and more things that I couldn't keep up with. Something about magical apartments and his friends I met earlier also being supernatural beings. But I was still trying to process the first thing he said. Hunter was a wolf shifter. *What did that mean?*

"Hunter?" I wanted to get his attention but he was in his own world.

"Rachael, I promise I will never hurt you. I don't think I could even if I tried. I'm serious. Please don't leave. I mean unless you really want to because I don't want to kidnap you for real. Benny said he would handle fixing your apartment and changing the lock to your door. I'm not sure if it's done but I could find out."

Before I realized what I was doing, my hands gripped Hunter's face and pulled him to me. My lips met his and the only thing I could hear was my heart pounding in my ears. It was a quick kiss, nothing to write home about, but it did the job. Hunter's eyes met mine and they were wide with surprise.

We stared at each other, my fingers intertwined in the strands of his beard. I really wanted to kiss him again. Longer this time.

Hunter cleared his throat and I dropped my hands to my lap. I squeezed my eyes shut as embarrassment turned my cheeks red. That was probably the stupidest impulse I had ever acted on. "I'm sorry."

The room was still, the soft hum of the air the only sound filling the space. My chest tightened with each passing second while I did my best to control my breathing. I expected to hear retreating footsteps, or feel the sharp sting of his hand.

Just when I was about to collapse into the bed and hide from the world, calloused hands gently cradled my cheeks. He tilted my head up as I blinked open my eyes. There was a fire in his gaze, one that had me clenching my thighs together. "I really need you to stop apologizing, sweetheart."

Then he was on top of me and the world melted away. The only thing that mattered was the way Hunter gathered me in his arms, my lips parting to allow his tongue to explore my mouth. He guided me backwards onto the bed and settled between my legs.

"Tell me to stop," he mumbled against my lips.

"Don't stop." I shook my head while my fingers threaded through his hair.

My eyes closed as I pulled Hunter back to me. He kissed down my neck, finding the sensitive spot behind my ear. One of his hands traveled down to the waistband of my pants. His fingers brushed along my skin, lighting a fire within my stomach. I let out a moan as Hunter bit down on my skin, scraping his teeth along the sensitive flesh.

"Rachael..." he growled. "Do you know what you do to me when you make sounds like that?" He pressed his hips into me as he went back to exploring my mouth and there was no mistaking it. I may have seen his cock earlier but there was no denying how huge it felt as it dug into my lower abdomen. Desire pooled between my legs and I wanted nothing more than for Hunter to discover it.

I was seconds from begging him for more when something licked my bare foot that was dangling from the bed. It felt like wet sandpaper rubbed over my skin. "What the hell?" Startled, I pulled my leg up, kneeing Hunter in the back of his thigh.

"What is it?" Hunter moved, sitting on the bed next to me, and peered over the edge of the bed. As I sat up onto my elbows, a black cat jumped onto the bed beside us. It stared at me for a second, green eyes peering into my soul, then strutted over my legs to sit in Hunter's lap. "How the fuck did you get in here, Thor?"

Hunter picked up the cat and dangled it in front of him. Thor let out a small set of meows as if he was actually answering Hunter's question. His eyes narrowed at the cat and I was convinced the two of them were actually having a conversation. Hunter sat Thor on the ground, pointing to the open bedroom door. "Well, leave the way you came, please."

We both tracked Thor as he walked out of the room, tail swishing through the air. When the black fur had disappeared fully, Hunter turned to me. "Sorry about that."

"I didn't know you had a cat." That was a stupid thing to say. I didn't know anything about this man before tonight.

"He isn't mine. Thor belongs to Benny, the redhead guy you saw earlier. But he's obsessed with me for some unknown reason and always finds a way into my apartment."

"Oh..." I tried to keep a straight face but failed. The absurdity of everything finally got to me. A laugh escaped and my hand flew up to cover my mouth. Hunter looked me up and down, a smile threatening the corners of his lips.

He gave in and we both fell back onto the bed, laughing until neither of us could breathe.

Some time later, I was wrapped in a blanket cocoon with a mug of delicious tea. There was a cheesy fall Hallmark movie playing on the TV. We had both slowly regained our composure earlier. Our conversation drifted to his apartment and I learned about the magical barrier that hid these units from the humans. It made sense. Even I could admit to being a bit nosy when I shouldn't be.

I could feel that Hunter was still holding things back. He was worried and that was understandable. After a bit of back and forth, I convinced Hunter that there was simply no way I was going to be able to fall asleep after all the excitement that just took place. Truthfully, my entire body felt sore and I was starving.

Hunter carried me to the couch and, as if he could read my mind, told me he would go make us some lunch. I offered to help but he told me not to move then came back with the large steaming mug. Sure, there was a small part of me that really liked being taken care of. But there was also the voice in the back of my head telling me I was lazy and unworthy of this treatment. It stood to reason that it sounded a lot like Chad telling me how useless of a girlfriend I was. I closed my eyes, hoping it would help stop the tears that were forming.

"Hey," Hunter pulled me from my thoughts. I opened my eyes and saw him crouching before me. He reached out, his thumb catching a stray tear that was running down my cheek. "Where'd ya go?"

"It's stupid," I half chuckled, trying to convince myself more than him.

"Nothing is stupid when it comes to what you're feeling."

No one had ever made me feel like my feelings mattered. I was so used to bottling it up and shoving it down that it felt weird for someone to actually make a point at giving me the space to talk.

"You're being really nice and I don't know why." Not exactly the whole truth, but I didn't want to ruin whatever Hunter and I had going on by bringing up my shitty excuse of an ex.

"I call this being a decent person." He tucked some loose hair behind my ear then stood. He grabbed a bowl from the coffee table in front of me and offered it to me. Inside it was some kind of soup that smelled heavenly. "It's chicken noodle. The best kind of soup to eat when you're sick."

"I'm not actually sick."

"Well you aren't healthy either. I feel like sick is an overarching term that covers a lot. I'd definitely refer to all of this," he waves to me in my bundle of blankets, "as sick." He swapped my nearly empty mug for the bowl then sat down sideways on the left side of the couch facing me.

Hunter still hadn't put on a shirt, not that I was necessarily complaining. He could go back to walking around naked if he really wanted to. I forced myself to focus on the bowl of soup in my hands instead of the half naked god beside me.

I brought a spoonful to my lips and the liquid slid down my throat easily. An involuntary moan slipped past my lips. It was hands down the best soup I had eaten in my life. Not even my grandma's recipes lived up to the foodgasm I had just experienced.

"Sweetheart..." In the middle of a bite, I turned my head to Hunter. His eyes were narrowed and the corners of his mouth twitched into a smile. He leaned towards me, his breath warming my chilled skin and causing goosebumps to form. "I'm going to need you to stop making that sound if you actually want to finish your food. We've already discussed what those moans of yours do to me."

When he pulled back, his gaze flickered between his lap and me. I looked down to where he had gestured and saw the unmistakable outline of his erection. My cheeks grew hot, a rush of warmth spreading across my face.

I hadn't thought it was loud enough to hear. But if the display before me was the effect I had on him, I would happily accept the consequences of my actions.

Setting my bowl on the table in front of me, I let the blanket wrapped around my shoulders fall. Confidence fueled my actions. I sat back and turned to Hunter.

"Kiss me."

"Are you sure? We really should talk more."

"I swear if you don't kiss me–" My sentence was cut off by his lips claiming mine. Any thoughts tumbling around my head immediately disappeared. One of his hands cradled the back of my head, but my skin was on fire, begging to be touched.

Hunter broke our kiss. He moved to my neck, running his teeth over my pressure point then kissing down to my collar bone. A low moan escaped from my lips and I didn't stop it.

He slid his free hand down my side, urging me back onto the couch. My head rested on one of the small pillows. He pulled back and kneeled over me. His eyes were wild while his lips pressed together in a line, forcing his breaths to come out harshly through his nose. A sense of pride rushed over me knowing that I was the one doing this to him.

"You're fucking gorgeous, Rachael." Both of his hands ran along my body, sliding over every curve.

My heart hammered in my chest. *Would he still feel that way when he saw the stretch marks?* While my thighs weren't toned by any means, they didn't have nearly as many as my stomach.

I breathed a silent sigh of relief though when his hands went to the sweatpants around my waist instead of my shirt. His fingers teased the waistband, sliding them down my hips. "Is this okay?"

I nodded, unable to form words. He pulled the fabric slowly down my legs and tugged it off. Then his hands kneaded my calves with expert fingers, working his way back up. I melted into the couch as more moans expressed my gratitude. When Hunter reached my knees, he pushed them apart and settled between them.

His hands danced over my thighs and up to my hips as he leaned over me, pressing a kiss to my lips. When he pulled away, he gazed down at me with desire in his eyes.

I reached up, running my fingers through the hair that covered his chest. I wanted this man. But was I ready for *all* of him?

"Hunter...?" I whispered.

"Yes, sweetheart?" His fingers caressed my thigh, causing my mind to go haywire.

"I... We... Us..." *What the hell was I trying to say?*

Hunter chuckled lightly. A single finger slid through the wetness that had gathered between my legs, spreading it up to my clit. He circled the sensitive nub with light pressure. My breath caught in my lungs as a wave of pleasure spread through my body.

"Right now is all about you. We don't have to do anything you aren't comfortable with. But I'm not going to lie and say that I don't want to hear what you sound like when I make you come."

He slipped a finger inside of me, my hips immediately bucking to meet his hand.

"So eager, sweetheart." He kissed along my jaw and I turned my head to give him better access. "Do you want me to make you come?" As he nipped down my neck, he added another finger and curled them inside me.

"Yes," I breathed, ready to combust after just a few strokes. It had been too long since someone took the time to explore my body and give me what I needed.

"Go on then, baby. Soak my hand." He stroked that spot inside me that not even I could reach and I saw stars. All thought left my head as Hunter worked me through my release. He pulled out his fingers and stuck them in his mouth, cleaning his fingers in the process.

"Hunter…" I trailed off, stopping myself before I could thank him for the mind-numbing orgasm. That would turn this from sexy to awkward real fast. I went to sit up, suddenly feeling the need to cover up, but Hunter's grip on my thighs stopped me.

"You taste like heaven, Rachael." He lowered himself to the couch, head between my legs. "And I'm fucking starving."

"Hunter, you–" I was cut off by his tongue licking from the base of my pussy to my clit. When he reached the sensitive bud, he pulled it into his mouth and circled it with his tongue. I squirmed underneath him, the sensations almost too much.

He held me down, his fingers digging into my thighs. Every swipe of his tongue sent a fresh flood of arousal between my legs. My fingers threaded through his hair. I was stuck between wanting to hold him in place so he would never stop or yanking him away because it was too much.

His teeth scraped my clit and I came undone. He fucked me with his tongue, lapping up every drop of my release. When he finally pulled away, my arms fell to my side. I looked up at Hunter to find his eyes shining, his lips turned up in a smile, and his clean cut beard glistening.

"I'll be right back." Hunter pressed his lips to my forehead. All I could do was offer a soft *hmm* in response. My arms and legs felt like limp noodles. I was still floating somewhere above us on cloud nine.

A wet cloth touched between my legs. My heart squeezed from the attention he was giving me. Not only had he just given me two mind blowing orgasms in the span of a few minutes, he did it all without any care for his own pleasure. That paired with this after care, I might never be able to leave this man.

When he had finished, Hunter gathered me in his arms and tucked me against him. He grabbed the forgotten blanket, draping it over the both of us. I rolled over to lay my head against his chest. My fingers ran through the hair that lined his pecs as he ran his hand along my spine.

My body relaxed further into his hold. I knew sleep would claim me at any moment. Right before it did, I heard Hunter whisper against my temple, "I'm falling really hard for you. I hope I don't screw this up."

CHAPTER FIVE
Hunter

Friday Night

When I forced my eyes open, the living room was blanketed in darkness. I groaned, my mind still waking up, and stretched out my stiff limbs. Falling asleep on the couch wasn't something I typically did, but then my senses woke up and Rachael's scent filled my nose.

I looked around the room for her. Short of the half-eaten bowl of soup on the coffee table, there was no trace of her. It was like I had imagined the last twenty-four hours.

Sitting up, I rubbed my face and blinked away the remaining bits of sleep. My stomach churned. *She left you, idiot.* We hadn't talked about everything, most importantly how she had been feeling. I was stupid to think she was okay with who I was.

I flopped back onto the couch, throwing my arm over my eyes. A groan powered by all built up frustration in my chest left my throat. Yes, I know I had brought this upon myself. I had fallen for the human.

Liliana and Benny were going to have a field day with this though. They'd be asking questions about where she went and what I did to scare her off. I would have to convince them that Rachael would keep our secret. Plus, if I left for my hunting trip now, I could forgo the party entirely and buy myself a few more days.

Anxiety coursed through my body. My wolf needed its release. Tomorrow was the full moon and I was pushing my luck. Shifting was natural to me. When I didn't do it, my skin felt like it was constantly crawling and, each day, it became a little harder to control the impulses.

The creak of a door followed by footsteps pulled me out of my thoughts. I lifted my arm and the breath caught in my lungs when I saw Rachael standing over me. Reaching behind me, I flicked on the end table lamp and the room was cast in a warm glow.

I looked back to Rachael who was smiling down at me. Relief flooded through me as my heart hammered away in my chest. Everything else was completely forgotten.

"Hey sleepyhead." Her hair was a mess, falling down in clumps around her face. She had on her oversized t-shirt and was still naked from the waist down. A fact I smiled to myself about. She was also putting weight on her injured foot which was a good sign. The tea Benny brewed for her had worked.

I sat up and pulled her into my lap. She laughed as she settled into me. The kind of laugh that could make a man addicted. Who was I kidding? This woman already had me wrapped around her finger and she didn't even know it.

"I thought you left," I muttered, not sure she even heard.

Rachael wrapped her arms around my neck and laid her head on my shoulder. I nuzzled my nose into her hair, soaking up the moment and memorizing every detail. The way her hair smelled. The way her body fit against mine, like a missing puzzle piece that I have spent forever searching for.

"Just had to use the bathroom," she whispered into my neck. "You looked so peaceful. I didn't want to wake you."

I tightened my hold on her, refusing to listen to my self-doubt telling me this was all a dream. One that I was bound to wake up from any moment.

"Hunter?" she asked.

"Yeah?" I mumbled into her hair.

"Were you planning on leaving for a trip or something?"

"What?" I pulled away, immediately missing the spicy scent of her shampoo.

She lifted her head and nodded towards the pile of bags near my front door. I had forgotten about them.

"Yeah, I had been. I go on a hunting trip once a month."

"Oh," she whispered. She moved to get off my lap and, as much as I wanted to keep her here where she belonged, I let her slide off and settle on the couch next to me. "Do you mean hunting or *hunting*?"

The way she said it the second time, a hint of innuendo with a raised eyebrow, told me she was smarter than I was giving her credit for.

"I think it's time we had more of a conversation, sweetheart." As much as I hated to say it, I knew it was time.

"Okay." She crossed her legs under her and sank into the couch, pulling the blanket onto her lap. If there was one thing I learned about her over the last twenty-four hours, she loved being cozy. I made a note to keep that blanket out on the couch for her. That is if she didn't immediately run for the hills after I told her everything.

"I don't know where to start." I ran my hand through my hair and scrubbed at my face, trying to figure out a way to say everything I needed to without scaring her. Then a soft hand rested on my knee. I met Rachael's gaze as she silently encouraged me.

"For generations, wolf shifters have been able to live among humans. We're able to control our shifting and, for the most part, nothing changes. I'm just really into red meat." Rachael let out a small laugh.

"Well, my great grandpa cheated on a witch when he was young. And she cursed our pack. We still have control of our shifting but we have to hunt during the full moon. Not humans, but other animals and such." I paused, debating on continuing. She needed to know the most important part of the curse.

Hunting wasn't optional. If we didn't do it on the full moon, then the next time we shifted would be our last. Our wolf instincts would take over and being around humans would end poorly. At least, that was what had been passed down for generations.

I took a deep breath, resigning to wait to tell her until after we had a little more time together. But the clock was running out and the moon was growing fuller. I shook my head to clear my mind. I could keep this secret to myself a little longer.

"It's always been a part of who I am," I sighed. "Liliana and Benny know about my monthly hunting trips but I've never told them the details. It's normal to me and telling other people makes it feel less so. It's easier just to keep this secret to myself, ya know?"

My heart was beating wildly in my chest. I forced myself to focus only on Rachael's hand, using the single point of contact to ground myself the best I could.

"Hunter, that's... I mean... Wow." She exhaled and squeezed my knee. My chest tightened with a mix of emotions: anxious, vulnerable, and even a little relieved. I may not have said everything that I should have but it was enough to feel like I wasn't carrying all the weight on my shoulders anymore.

"I know this is a lot and I wouldn't blame you if you needed some space. Or whatever. I don't expect you to just accept all of this." Her hand left my knee and I drew in a quick breath, expecting her to leave.

Instead, she climbed on top of me and straddled my legs. Her hands cupped my face. She kissed me, the softest of kisses. When she sat back, her eyes shone in the soft light.

"I'm not going anywhere," she whispered.

"But…"

"Hunter, I'm not going anywhere. Thank you for trusting me with this piece of you. Truthfully, I always felt like something drew me to this place. I've always believed there was *more* out there. And now, I've found it."

I crashed my lips into hers, my hands sliding under her shirt to grip her bare hips. Her fingers threaded through my hair and tugged at my roots. She moaned into my mouth as I ran my thumbs along the inside of her thighs. I swallowed every sound and relished in the way her body responded to me.

"Shit, Rachael," I growled, grabbing her wrists and tugging them away from my hair. "You're making it really fucking hard to be a gentleman right now."

"Then don't."

"Are you sure?" She nodded in response but it wasn't enough. I wanted to hear it from those pretty lips of hers. "I need you to say the words, sweetheart."

"Fuck me, Hunter. Please."

"It will be my pleasure." I slid my hands under her ass and stood. My lips found hers once more, exploring every inch of her mouth as she pressed herself against my chest.

Somehow, I made it into the bedroom without injury. My shins hit the mattress and I lowered Rachael to the sheet. She laid back, her hair falling out from her bun and framing her face. Her cheeks were flushed, presumably from our short make out session.

My hands moved from the globes of her ass to the front of her thighs. I enjoyed the soft moans that left her lips as my thumbs worked into her tense muscles.

"Hunter, please," Rachael whined as she looked up at me through hooded eyes. I smiled to myself.

It was time to show this goddess of a woman what it felt like to be with a proper man.

Chapter Six

Rachael

When I told Hunter to fuck me, I had meant with his cock, not his eyes. His gaze roamed over my body as he stood between my legs and, in that moment, I wanted to cover up. My t-shirt simply didn't feel like enough.

Hunter's hands moved from my thighs up to the hem of my shirt. As he started to tug it up, my hands flew down to keep it in place. Sex with my ex did not include all this fanfare. Typically, our clothes stayed on. It was lackluster at best.

"Rachael..." he growled, my name a warning.

"Hunter– I'm not– I don't look like you." The words came out rushed and as soon as I said them, Hunter's eyes darkened. My heart hammered in my chest as my cheeks warmed with embarrassment.

"I could care less what you look like under these clothes. Your body is perfect just the way it is and deserves to be worshiped. I will spend as much time as needed doing just that until you believe it." The fire in his eyes dared me to contradict what he said.

I was emboldened by his words, feeling for the first time that I was actually worthy of desire from a man like him. I let his hands snake under the fabric, goosebumps trailing his touch.

I relaxed into the bed and my eyes fluttered shut. Hunter's expert fingers ran along my curves, trailing over every stretch mark. For the first time in forever, I was okay with a man seeing me. All of me. These marks were part of who I was and told the story of what I had overcome.

Hunter grabbed the bottom of my shirt, slowly lifting it and guiding my arms up as he did. He stopped when the fabric was gathered around my wrists and expertly wrapped the shirt around itself.

My eyes flew open as I tested my makeshift restraint. If I tried hard enough, I could free myself. I sucked in deep breaths through my nose. But I wanted this, more than I could ever explain. It wasn't fear coursing through my veins making it hard to breathe. It was arousal. I was so turned on and desperate to be touched.

"Since you have such a hard time letting me enjoy your body however I want," he whispered into my ear, "I think I'll keep you like this for a bit." He nipped at the sensitive skin behind my ear.

"But if it's too much, tell me. Just say 'red' and I'll stop. Okay?" I nodded my head, not trusting my voice. "No, sweetheart. I need words."

"Yes, Hunter."

"What's the word?"

"Red."

"Good girl." Hunter's hands ran along my skin, down my arms, to my breasts. He held them in his palms and lifted them gently so they sat next to each other on my chest. His fingers worked my nipples, pinching and rolling them until there were firm peaks.

"Fuck..." I groaned through clenched teeth. My bound hands flew to his head, my fingers running through his hair.

"Now, now, sweetheart," Hunter tsked. He grabbed my wrists and pinned them with one hand above my head.

Arousal flooded my center as he sucked a nipple into his mouth. It was too much and not enough, all at the same time. I tried to clench my thighs together, to provide enough friction to give myself some relief. It was a useless attempt with Hunter between my legs.

As if reading my mind, his free hand slid down my body. Expert fingers slipped through my wetness, swirling it around my clit then dipping into my center. "Shit, sweetheart. Is all of this for me?"

I could feel my release building with each pass. The rhythm was intoxicating, my body wanting more.

"Are you going to come for me?" I nodded, unable to form words. I was so close to the edge. A gasp filled the space between us.

Hunter claimed my nipple with his mouth once more, sucking and licking the sensitive nub. I ached to run my hand through his hair but his hand on my bondage held strong. He pressed two fingers into me, working my clit with his thumb and pushing me closer to my release. It was right there. I pressed my hips up into his hand, matching the rapid strokes until I was teetering on the edge.

"That's it, baby. Ride my hand. Find your release." He pushed a third finger into me as his teeth clamped down on my nipple and it was all I needed. With one final buck of my hips, I plummeted over the edge. Hunter pressed his chest into mine, kissing me as his fingers worked me through my release.

Hunter slowed his pace as my body relaxed and when he pulled his hand away, a chill ran through my body. I missed his warmth immediately.

I watched through hooded eyes as Hunter brought his hand up to his mouth and licked my release from his fingers. *God, this man.* He stood shirtless at my feet and I couldn't help letting my eyes roam over his body.

We hadn't turned on any lights but the moon shone through the open blinds, bathing the room in a soft glow. It was much more enjoyable to take in his muscular features when I wasn't on the verge of an emotional breakdown because I hurt myself.

My gaze followed the trail of hair along his chest down his abdomen. Unfortunately, this time it disappeared beneath the waistband of his shorts. An ache pulsed between my legs at the sight of the bulge of his cock. I tugged my bottom lip between my teeth, hoping Hunter wasn't going to make me beg. Though I gladly would. I would do anything this man asked me.

"Like what you see?" His question pulled me from my dirty thoughts and my eyes met his once again.

"You're a bit overdressed," I smirked.

"That can be fixed." He hooked his thumbs in his waistband and pushed his shorts off his hips. My mouth watered seeing his bobbing cock once again. I had no idea how it was going to fit inside me but I didn't care.

I barely felt his hands as they gripped my thighs. "Ready for the fun to begin, sweetheart?" He chuckled, not waiting for a response before he pushed me up the bed. The sheets tightened under my skin as I slid along them. Hunter stopped when my bound wrists hit the headboard, my head resting under them.

Hunter crawled up the bed and stopped with his hands on either side of my head. He pressed his lips to mine, a gentle kiss. One that expressed that all of this was more than just lust.

Leaving me breathless, he sat back on his heels and ran his hands down my body. He lingered for a moment on the stretch marks on my stomach, tracing the skin with his fingers.

"You are fucking gorgeous, Rachael. No matter what anyone else says. Even me. All that matters is how you feel." He ran his lips along the prominent marks, nipping at the skin every so often. "And you deserve to feel like the absolute queen you are."

Fuck, Hunter's mouth alone was going to be the end of me. The way he talked to me, how special he made me feel. Not to mention what he could do with it between my legs.

He reached over me to grab a silver package from his nightstand. He tore it open with his teeth then rolled the condom down his length. Then his thumb circled my clit, sending sparks of pleasure through my core. The pressure built between my legs once more and I needed him inside me.

My legs wrapped around his back as my hands went to his chest.

"Eager are we?" He chuckled, pinning my hands above my head.

"Hunter, please." I begged. His touch was torturous, keeping me on the edge.

"I'm going to need both of my hands for this, sweetheart. Be a good girl and keep yours above your head. Don't make me tie you to my bed frame." *Was that a threat or a promise?*

"Yes, sir," I said mockingly but the fire in Hunter's eyes told me he loved it.

He pushed the tip of his cock against my entrance and I gasped at the sudden intrusion. He went slow, each inch a delicious torture as he pulled out and pushed back in. Each time he went a little further, a whimper left my lips as my fists balled into the sheet above me.

"Shh, baby. Relax. I've got you." Hunter pulled my nipple into his mouth, sucking and biting then giving the other the same attention. He alternated between them and kept the same heavenly pressure on my clit.

His balls met my ass and I knew he was bottomed out. Somehow, Hunter felt even larger inside me. He stopped his movements, letting me adjust to his size.

"Ready?" he asked and I nodded, biting my bottom lip to keep from making too many feral sounds. "Words, baby."

"Yes, Hunter. Fuck me." I whispered. And boy, did he fuck me. He pulled out, leaving just the tip inside me then slammed into me. I tasted copper as I bit down on my lip to keep from screaming. He continued pumping inside me and it was like his cock expanded by the second. It was stretching me in the best possible way, filling me more than I ever thought possible.

"I'm almost there, Rachael," Hunter groaned. I was right there with him. His thumb circled my clit harder, pushing me towards the edge with him. "Come with me, baby."

He bit down on my nipple and tugged at it, pain mixing with pleasure. That was all I needed. A scream I barely recognized as my own filled the room. Hunter bucked his hips and fucked me through my orgasm as wave after wave of pleasure crashed through my body.

"Fuck, Rachael," he grunted my name as he chased his own release. It was almost uncomfortable, the pressure inside me, but I was lost in a sea of orgasms.

Hunter stilled as both of us fought to catch our breath. He pressed his lips to mine. A gentle kiss that was completely opposite of the rough fucking that had just taken place. My chest squeezed with more emotions than I could even try to identify in my post orgasmic haze. It was such a domesticated gesture, one that should feel wrong coming from someone who I've known for barely twenty-four hours.

But something told me I was exactly where I was meant to be.

Hunter nuzzled into my neck, rubbing his nose along the sensitive skin. As much as I enjoyed the comforting weight of him above me and the warmth radiating from his body onto mine, my shoulders were growing uncomfortable.

"Um, Hunter? Are you going to get up?"

"Nope."

I giggled as he nipped at my neck, sending goosebumps across my skin. "No? And why not?"

"Well, I can't."

"Can't?" My chest tightened as the post-orgasm haze wore off.

"I should have warned you ahead of time, sweetheart." Hunter reached up as he spoke and freed my wrists from their restraints. He pulled each wrist to his lips before kissing my forehead.

"Warned me about what?" I asked. My heart skipped my beat.

"My knot." He brushed a few stray strands of hair out of my face before then shifted his weight to his forearms. The confusion must have been written all over my face because Hunter continued. "Most canid species have them, a knot that is. It was the one thing wolf shifters didn't lose as we evolved." I arched my brows in question, still very unsure what he was talking about.

"It's tissue at the base of my cock." The wheels turned in my head, remembering the way his penis looked when I was drooling over it last night. I had too quickly dismissed the extra thickness in my lust-filled state.

How the fuck was I so oblivious?

He chuckled and kissed the tip of my nose. The gesture caused my body to relax. "When I have sex, it expands kind of like a balloon so nothing can leak out."

"Excuse me?" I felt flushed. By leak out, did he mean...?

"It keeps my sperm inside to help with um, well... breeding."

What a second, did he mean breeding as in children? And why did that excite me?

"Sweetheart, I need you to relax that sweet pussy of yours. Otherwise, the swelling will never go down."

"Oh, sorry!" I hadn't realized I had clenched down, but as I took stock of what was going on between my legs, Hunter's cock was subtly pulsing inside me. Taking a breath through my nose, I did my best to calm the panic threatening to overpower the post-orgasm bliss. "Okay. This is fine. So um, how long do we have to stay like this?" It was absolutely not fine. My whole body was starting to feel increasingly uncomfortable as I was forced to lay underneath him.

"It shouldn't be too long. A few minutes. Just needs to go down enough so I can pull out without hurting you."

"Okay..." *Fuck, why was this so awkward?* The longer I laid there, letting the thoughts tumble around in my mind unspoken, the more the panic took hold. My shoulders tensed and I forced my eyes closed as the back of my throat burned. I didn't want to cry in front of Hunter. Especially not with his cock lodged inside me.

What felt like hours was only minutes, probably even seconds. I couldn't even put a pin on what emotions I was feeling. Contentment warmed my body, but regret flooded my mind. Well, maybe not regret but definitely anxiety. I was overwhelmed.

"Shit." Hunter kissed my forehead and cupped my cheek with one of his hands. "Hey, it's okay. I'm right here." A tear slid down my cheek as I blinked away the painful pressure behind my eyes. Hunter gently swiped it away. A shiver ran down my spine causing my body to shake.

Hunter's brows furrowed and his shoulders tensed as he looked down at me. His thumb brushed over my skin, helping to soothe my frayed nerves.

"Take deep breaths with me. In through your nose. Out through your mouth." He exaggerated his breaths and I rested my hands on his chest, focusing on the rise and fall to help steady my breathing.

"I'm so sorry, sweetheart. I should have warned you. I seriously fucked this up." There was something genuine to his voice, like he actually cared about my wellbeing. Something my fucked up ex never bothered to do.

Because he isn't your ex.

As I chastised myself for once again thinking about my ex, Hunter shifted his weight. He pushed himself up onto his palms "I think I can pull out now. It may be uncomfortable at first but let me know if it hurts." I nodded.

Slowly, he sat back on his heels, keeping his eyes on me to gauge my reaction. There wasn't any pain and the only discomfort came when his cock was no longer inside me. The emptiness was a stark contrast to the knot that had filled me only seconds ago.

"I'll be right back," he whispered. I closed my eyes and hummed in response, unable to find my voice. The bed shifted as he left and I missed the warmth of his body immediately.

The sound of the shower turning on came from the bathroom. A slight chill settled over my skin as I rolled over to my side and debated on getting up to join Hunter. My stiff muscles would benefit greatly from a hot shower, but I was sinking into the comfort of the bed with every passing second. Before I could make the decision, I was being lifted off the bed by two very strong arms.

My eyes flew open and I threw my arms around Hunter's neck. Looking up, the corners of his lips were turned up in smirk as he carried me from the bedroom to the bathroom.

"You know, a girl could get used to this kind of treatment," I joked, laying my head on his shoulder.

Hunter carefully maneuvered us through the door frame and towards the toilet. He set me down on the open seat, kissed the top of my head, then stepped back. My heart hammered in my chest as I looked up at Hunter.

He smiled down at me. I think I was falling for this man. I knew it was crazy, absolutely bonkers, but I didn't care. It all just felt right.

"Pee. Shower. Bed. In that order." Hunter kneeled at my feet as he spoke. I relieved myself as he lifted my wrapped foot and rested it on top of his thigh. He unwrapped it then straightened out my leg so he could inspect the sole.

"The stitches look okay. No swelling or redness. Does it hurt at all?" I shook my head.

"Alright. Finish up and then let's see if you can stand, okay?" After cleaning up, he offered me his hand and I gingerly stood, ignoring the fact I hadn't washed my hands. I kept most of my weight on my good foot, afraid to push my luck too far. "Come on, sweetheart. I've got you."

I took a step forward, putting weight on the stitches, and was pleasantly surprised when there was no pain. There was some pressure, but nothing compared to the pain I had experienced when it happened.

"What is this magic?" I chuckled.

"The tea you had before lunch. Benny brewed it. He's a kitchen witch. Specializes in brewing. I won't even begin to understand it all but he knows what he's doing." Hunter wrapped an arm around my waist. One small step at a time, he guided me to the shower.

Stepping into the shower, I keep my weight on my toes. It was probably best not to set my foot down all the way. The hot water felt heavenly on my skin. It melted away all of the trauma from the past twenty-four hours. I closed my eyes and let everything wash down the drain.

Hunter stepped in behind me, using his expert fingers to wash my hair and massage my scalp. Moans fell from my lips. I was in bliss. He worked his way down my body, his hands working my tight muscles. I leaned my back to his chest and let the water flow down my stomach.

His lips found my ear, kissing the skin before whispering, "You did such a good job, sweetheart. You took me so well." My head lolled back on his shoulder. I basked in his praise, his words warming my skin in a way the hot water couldn't.

His hand traveled along my stomach as he encouraged my legs apart with his. My ass found a seat on his thigh and his fingers spread me open until the water was running over my swollen clit. The water was feather-light but the heat was intense. I didn't think it would have been possible but my insides clenched, begging for another orgasm.

"Hunter," I whined, wanting him to touch me.

"Does my greedy cunt want to come again already, baby?" His words were a growl in my ear, sending goosebumps down my spine. His free hand came up to my throat and pressed against my jaw, keeping my head pinned backwards and my neck exposed.

"Yes. Please." He circled my clit with a single finger, giving me the pressure I so desperately needed. He ran his teeth over my pressure point, biting down at the column of my neck.

"Fuck, Hunter!" I choked, coming undone from all the sensations. Riding out my orgasm on his thigh, I pushed my clit into his hand. My body was weightless and my head was spinning. I was dizzy from the high and I never wanted to come down.

"I thought your laugh was my favorite sound in the world. Turns out, it's the way you moan my name when I'm making you come." I hummed in response, my body leaning against him. His chest shook as he laughed.

"Come on, sweetheart. Let's get you to bed." He lifted me into his arms and I snuggled into his chest, not caring about the wet hair sticking against my cheek. Somewhere between the bathroom and bedroom, I let sleep claim me, feeling safe and protected in Hunter's arms.

CHAPTER SEVEN
Hunter

Saturday Morning

The sun was just starting to peek through the blinds, casting light directly into my face. I cursed my forgetfulness for not closing them last night. It felt like I had just closed my eyes. I had at least a few more hours of sleep left in me.

A soft hum vibrated across my chest. I looked down at Rachael, who was curled up on my chest with my arm wrapped around her shoulders. She had practically passed out in my arms in the shower after our fun. I felt a sense of pride that I was able to do that.

My wolf had wanted her, demanded her. As soon as my cock had felt her warmth, there was no going back. Giving into my primal instincts may have pushed her too far. I resigned myself to the fact that I would have to beg her for forgiveness and hope she didn't see me in the same light as her jackass of an ex.

She looked so peaceful as she slept. Those pinched lines between her eyebrows disappeared and her shoulders were relaxed. Not to mention how fucking sexy she looked in the clean shirt of mine that I slipped over her body. Her hair fanned out on one of my pillows.

Carefully, I removed myself from under Rachael and stalked towards the window. My sleep schedule had already been screwed up before this weekend, but it seemed to be even worse.

The full moon was tonight. If I didn't shift, didn't hunt, there was no telling what would happen. My father instilled the fear of the curse in me, just like his father did to him, and so on. My skin crawled with the need to shift. The craving for copper to coat my tongue was so strong it made me nauseous.

But if I didn't give in, would I actually lose my humanity, unable to fight off the animal instincts?

"Hunter?" Rachael's sleep-filled voice found me, pulling me from my deepest thoughts.

I closed the blinds then turned. Rachael reached out, her eyes blinking at me as if trying to decide if she was still sleeping. I adjusted the sweatpants on my hips then slipped in next to her and pulled her against me. She wrapped her leg around mine, nuzzling into my side. I buried my nose into her hair and breathed her in. She still smelled like herself even after our shower. I didn't know how it was possible but I didn't question it.

Rachael's fingers slipped over the hair on my chest. Maybe I hadn't fucked things up too badly after all. I mean, if she was reaching for me while on the edge of sleep, she had to feel content.

Her thumb brushed lightly at my skin, tracing the ink on my upper arm, and there was a calming effect to her movements. My eyes closed. For the first time this week, my mind was quiet.

"Hunter," Rachael whispered. I groaned, covering her body with mine. "Hunter!"

"Shhh, go back to sleep, sweetheart."

"It's almost noon, Hunter. And I need the bathroom!" She giggled and pushed at my chest. Instead of letting her up, I rolled over and pinned her under me with my hips.

The tip of my nose ran up her neck as my hand worked the hem of her shirt up past her breasts. I took a nipple into my mouth, sucking until it was a solid peak, then turned my attention to the other. Little moans of pleasure escaped Rachael's mouth.

"Hunter, I really need to pee," she protested, but I didn't stop. Sliding my hand between her legs, I slipped a finger into her already wet pussy then added another.

"But you're already so wet for me, baby. I can't deny my greedy girl what she so obviously wants." I brushed my thumb over her clit, eliciting a string of expletives as Rachael tried not to give into my touch. "Plus, aren't full bladders supposed to make orgasms more intense?"

"Where the fuck did you hear that?" She ran her nails along my scalp and I moaned at the sensation.

"I don't know, but why don't we test the theory?" I claimed her lips with a rough kiss, pushing my tongue into her mouth to deepen it further. She held me to her with a tug of my hair.

I pumped my fingers into her and used the leaking arousal to continue torturing her clit. She arched her back, pushing herself down onto my hand. I wrapped my hand around her throat and could feel the blood pounding through her veins. It was taking every ounce of control to not bite into her neck. My wolf wanted a taste, demanded it.

Memories of my teeth sinking into the necks of hares and deer flooded my mind. The way the warm blood danced across my tongue and sent my senses into overdrive. The way their bodies twitched under my paws as the adrenaline coursed through my veins and I tore their flesh away from their bones.

Shit. I shook the thoughts from my head. I needed to focus on Rachael, on giving her all my attention. If I did that, then everything would be okay. I could fight the instincts.

Rachael looked up at me through hooded eyes. Her lips parted slightly and she gasped as I twisted my wrist and pulled her earlobe between my teeth. "Fuck, sweetheart. Your pussy is clenching around my fingers."

She moaned, moving her hips in search of more friction. I squeezed the sides of her throat, putting pressure on her artery to restrict the flow of blood to her brain. Her eyes went wide as she looked up at me. It wasn't fear in her eyes though, it was lust.

"Two fingers inside you and my greedy pussy still wants more." She tried to speak, but all that came out was a broken gasp as I applied a fraction more pressure to her throat and clit. "Tell me what I want to hear, baby."

"Please, sir," she forced out. "Make me come." I curled my fingers inside her, hitting the spot I knew would make her fall apart under me.

A strangled scream fell from her lips and I claimed her mouth, swallowing every sound as my tongue danced with hers. Her legs shook underneath me as I worked Rachael through her release. When she finally stilled, I loosened my hold on her neck and removed my fingers from inside her.

I pulled away, looking down at the beautiful woman beneath me. A blush crept along her cheeks as I tucked a stray piece of hair behind her ear. "You doing okay?"

"Mhmm. I, um–" She closed her eyes and laughed. "I think we just proved the theory correct."

While I enjoyed my hunting trips in the sense that they felt normal, this weekend was turning out to be more than I ever dreamed. If I had known all I had to do to feel this overwhelming comfort of domestic life was break down Rachael's door and kick out her shitty boyfriend, I would have done it a long time ago.

After our little adventure this morning, I helped her to the bathroom. By helping, I meant I carried her even though I knew she wanted to protest. After setting her down on the toilet, she demanded I give her some privacy to get ready for the day. I only agreed after making her promise she would call for me if she needed help. She kissed me on the cheek and my chest tightened at the simple action.

I left her to do whatever she needed, slipping on a clean shirt and leaving one on the bathroom vanity for her. The sound of the water bouncing off the tile drifted through my apartment as I worked on preparing us a late breakfast. I listened for any sign of distress, wanting to be available to Rachael in an instant if she needed me. Everything sounded normal so I returned to the task at hand.

Sausage links cooked on the stove while I whipped up waffle batter. There wasn't much in the way of food since I had expected to be gone on my trip by now and typically went to the store before coming home. There was some leftover soup but I would feel bad if I didn't offer Rachael some variety. I was preheating my waffle iron when I heard Rachael release a hiss from behind me. Turning around, I found her limping slowly towards the kitchen, favoring her injured foot.

"Damn it, baby. Why didn't you call for me?" I scooped her up, setting her down on the kitchen counter. Dropping to my knee, I inspected the stitches on the bottom of her foot. Nothing was swollen and the stitches were still in place. "Does it hurt? I should have been more careful this morning." I stood up, turning to leave. "Let me go get bandages and some ibuprofen. Then I can brew you some more tea. I should have never let you–"

Rachael grabbed my arm, effectively shutting up my brain. She pulled me to her and I settled between her knees. Her face was inches from mine. I wanted to kiss her, but if I did, breakfast would go uneaten.

She didn't get the memo though, her fingers slipping through my beard to cup my jaw. Our lips met in a soft kiss, the kind two lovers have after a long day.

Lovers.

Yeah, I thought maybe I was falling in love with Rachael.

"Hi," she whispered against my lips then pulled away. The sun filtering through the kitchen bounced off the countertop surrounding her in a halo of light.

"Hi," I responded, unable to say or do anything else. She smiled at me, running her nails along my jaw. Chills ran down my back and groans of pleasure escaped from the back of my throat as she worked her way under my chin. She giggled as my whole body practically vibrated with pleasure. I was seconds away from shaking my foot like a damn dog.

She pulled her hands away and my body immediately missed her touch. I kissed her forehead, knowing if I did anything else I wouldn't have the self control to stop myself. My wolf wanted to come out and play.

"Are those waffles?" She looked over my shoulder and eyed the plate of golden brown delights that I had stacked up. The sausage rested on the back of the stove.

"Sure are. Hungry?"

"Starving."

"Let me just finish up these last few and then I'll make us plates." I turned away, opening the waffle maker and grabbing the batter.

"I can help!" As I spun to tell her that it wasn't necessary, she slid off the counter, seeming to forget about her foot bothering.

In the mess of trying to keep her on the counter and not dumping waffle mix all over us, my forearm slammed against the hot surface of the waffle maker.

"Fuck!" I gritted my teeth to keep from losing my shit as I wrapped my uninjured arm around Rachael's waist. The smell of burnt hair lingered in the air as I set Rachael on her feet.

"Shit, Hunter!" She grabbed my wrist, examining the pattern of reddening skin up my arm. "Here, let's cool it down." She pulled me towards the sink, turned it on, and thrust the offending appendage under the barely cool water.

"Sweetheart, I'm fine." I tried to pull my arm from her grasp but her nails dug into my skin. She shot me a look that had a shiver running down my spine. The last time someone looked at me like that was when I was an unruly child.

She turned her attention back to caring for the burn. Her fingers along my skin soothed what little pain there was more than the water. I didn't have the heart to tell her that I healed faster than humans. Even as we stood there, the once angry burn was probably no worse than a low grade sunburn now.

My gaze was fixed on her face. Her brows furrowed together in concentration as she turned off the water and patted my skin dry with a paper towel. Her bottom lip pulled between her teeth while she inspected my arm.

Is this what it felt like to have someone care for me?

My heart leapt in my chest, my stomach following suit. Three little words threatened to ruin all of this.

"We might want to put some aloe or something on it. It doesn't look as bad as I thought it was." She met my gaze and I knew I looked like a fool. A lovesick teenager. "What? Why are you looking at me like that?"

"No one has ever taken care of me before. Not since my mom anyway." I brushed my knuckles along her cheek and she leaned into the touch.

"Well, I'm here now," she whispered, turning her head to kiss my wrist. Whether she knew it or not, her words just solidified what I already knew. This woman was mine.

She dropped her gaze down to my arm and her eyes went wide. "Um, Hunter? Where's the burn?"

I looked to find freshly healed skin. The only evidence of the incident was a few hairless patches. I chuckled, having expected this. "I did try to tell you, sweetheart. I heal fast. It's a wolf thing."

"Of course it is," she huffed, dropping my arm.

"Besides, I'm more worried about you right now. How's your foot?"

"Completely forgot about it." She gave it a little wiggle. "Eh, it feels fine. At least for now."

"Well, let's not push our luck anymore." I left the kitchen, heading to the bathroom to grab the ibuprofen. When I returned, Rachael was perched on the counter tearing apart one of the waffles.

"Couldn't wait, huh?" I offered her two pills and a bottle of water from the fridge. She happily took both, swallowing the remaining waffle before taking the medicine.

"I told you I was starving!"

"Never doubted you for a second, sweetheart." I grabbed a waffle of my own then found my place between Rachael's legs. It was quickly becoming one of my favorite places. I rested a hand on her thigh and kissed her on the forehead. She smiled, her nose crinkling as she did. It was one of the most wonderful sights in the world.

We stayed in the kitchen, munching our way through our cold breakfast. I tried to keep my hands to myself as we chatted, exchanging our likes and dislikes much like a couple on a first date. We had skipped past the conversation part yesterday after all. I could listen to her talk all day. The enthusiasm she expelled over the smallest things was contagious. She could be telling me about the history of concrete and she would still have my full attention.

It was hard not to let my hand wander while I listened. Rachael's skin was so soft, so welcoming. I slipped under the hem of her shirt, my thumb circling her hip. She stumbled over her words. My knuckles skimmed up her side and I soaked in the way her skin pebbled under my touch.

"Is this your way of shutting me up?" she muttered.

"Never. It's just been too long since I touched you." I pressed my chest against her, kissing down her neck. Her heartbeat pulsed in my mouth as I dragged my teeth along her pressure point. Her tiny moans nearly had me losing control. Images of claws digging into her perfect skin flashed in my mind, leaving behind fresh marks of crimson.

"This is a little more than just touching, Hunter," Rachael whispered into my ear. *She was right.* Fear gripped my stomach from my earlier thoughts. I pulled away, dropping my hands and shoving my fists into the pockets of my sweatpants.

"I'm sorry. I should have asked." I dropped my head, staring at my bare feet on the kitchen tile. I was forcing myself on her. My shame from yesterday's lack of communication reared its ugly head. The fear that I would hurt her was at the forefront of my mind.

"Hey," Rachael whispered. Her fingers held onto my chin, tilting my head up to her. The features of her face were soft with the corners of her mouth turned up in a small smile. "You don't have to apologize, Hunter. I trust you."

"You do?"

"Yes. I feel safe with you." She cupped my face and I covered her hands with mine. I let her touch calm the raging war inside me.

"I don't want you to ever think I would take advantage of that. You deserve the world, Rachael."

"And I know you'll give it to me." She pressed her lips to mine. A silent promise. I closed my eyes, drinking her in and letting her set the pace.

She pulled me to her and pressed her hips into me. My cock was already standing at attention, ready to give her whatever she wanted. I knew she felt what she was doing to me when she moaned into my mouth. Her fingers raked through my hair, her nails digging into my shoulders.

Her sounds were edging me on. All I wanted to do was sink into her perfect pussy. But I couldn't get carried away, not with the full moon tonight and my wolf itching to be freed.

When she pulled away, we were both panting, unable to catch our breath. Her fists balled my t-shirt, keeping my chest against hers. Our hearts raced in time with each other.

"Hunter, please," she whispered between breaths.

"Baby, I'm going to need you to tell me exactly what you want."

"Take me to bed?"

"Fuck yes."

CHAPTER EIGHT
Rachael

This man. This fucking man.

He woke up a part of me I hadn't known existed. The way he touched my body, gentle yet possessive, had me ready to combust. I needed this man and I wasn't sure how I felt about that.

Hunter carried me to the bedroom with ease, sitting me down on the mattress. His hands moved to the hem of my shirt, but I stopped him, sinking to my knees. My hands slid up his thighs and his muscles contracted under my touch. My eyes roamed over his gray sweatpants that did nothing to hide the impressive bulge between his legs.

"Rachael?" His fingers grasped my chin and tilted my head up. "You don't have to do this."

"I want to, Hunter." My hands moved up to the waistband of his sweatpants. I slipped my fingers beneath the fabric, pulling it down his hips and freeing his hard cock. "I want to make you feel as good as you make me feel. I want to take care of you."

I wrapped my hand around the base of his cock, just above his knot, giving it small pumps while my mouth circled the tip.

"Fuck, baby." He threaded his fingers through my hair at the top of my neck and gripped it. The motion sent electricity down my spine, my insides throbbing with need. I clenched my thighs together in an attempt to relieve some of the building pressure between my legs.

I took him further into my mouth, running my tongue along the vein on the underside of his cock. His moans of pleasure urged me on as I continued my torturous speed of licking up and down his shaft.

"Sweetheart, I need to fuck this pretty throat of yours," Hunter muttered from above me. "If you don't want that, you better stop now." He loosened his hold on my hair as he pulled out and rested the tip of his cock on my tongue.

I nodded, ready to take whatever he gave me. I wondered if I looked as sexy as I felt. I was on my knees for a man, something I never thought I would do willingly, but I felt empowered.

I was in control.

Chad had always made me feel guilty if I didn't suck him off. He whined about it not being fair as if he ever went down on me. That asshole was the definition of a man child and I had no idea how I lasted in a relationship with him for as long as I did.

His fingers wrapped around my throat, forcing my head up to meet his gaze. The fire in his eyes sent a fresh flood of arousal between my legs. "Stay out of that pretty little head and use your fucking words, baby."

I smirked up at him, knowing what he wanted but refusing to give it to him. Pushing into his hand, I licked up the precum that had gathered on the tip of his cock. The saltiness danced across my taste buds as it mixed with the spit gathering in my mouth.

"Rachael." My name came out as a warning, sending my stomach into knots in the best possible way. His eyes darkened as he looked down at me, but it didn't stop me.

I opened my mouth, allowing the saliva to slide from my tongue and onto his length. My tongue teased the head of his cock, while my fingers wrapped around his knot. He let out a low moan as I massaged the swelling tissue.

It pulsed beneath my touch and I sucked him into my mouth, moaning as he slid along my tongue. His hips bucked into me, hitting the back of my throat and causing me to gag slightly before he pulled out.

A growl was the only warning I had before his grip tightened on my throat, a small whimper barely able to escape. My vision darkened on the edges as he pushed me back and off him, my hands falling into my lap. I was sitting back on my heels when he loosened his grip. "You want to be a brat, baby? Now you get to beg me."

His cock bobbed in front of me, teasing me. It glistened with my saliva. His knot widened and my insides clenched remembering how it stretched me.

Fuck, I wanted this. I wanted him.

"Please, sir," I whined. He glared down at me, his darkened eyes telling me everything I needed to know. My heart hammered in my chest. "Fuck my throat with your cock."

"Put your hands behind your back and leave them there," he demanded as he released my throat. I clasped my hands together behind me and the position forced my chest forward. His fingers threaded through my hair once more, fisting it and forcing my head back to look at him. "If it's too much, bring your hands up. Okay?"

"Yes, sir." I barely got the words out before he pushed his cock into my mouth, only stopping when he hit the back of my throat. He held me in place as I instinctively tried to push off of him. It was hard to breathe, my nose pressed into his pelvis and his knot lodged against my mouth.

"Relax, baby. Breathe." I did as he said, relaxing my throat and breathing through my nose. I arched my back to give my arms more room as I clenched my hands together in a fist.

"Good girl." He pulled out slowly, drool falling from the corner of my mouth. His thumb brushed it away. "Such a good fucking girl."

I breathed through my nose as he slowly fucked my mouth. Saliva gathered on my tongue as he pumped in and out, coating him as he picked up speed. Hunter moaned and his grip in my hair tightened.

"Fuck, baby. Your mouth feels so fucking good. You take me so well." He slammed into me over and over, my body warming from his praise. Involuntary tears fell down my face and Hunter swiped them away with his thumb. I wanted to touch myself but I didn't want this to stop. I had never felt this empowered, knowing I was the one making Hunter moan and lose control the way he was.

"Sweetheart, I'm so fucking close. Are you going to be a good girl for me and swallow?" His thumb traced along my jaw, waiting for my answer.

All I could offer was a slight nod of my head, but that was all it took. Seconds later, warm spurts of come shot down my throat and I struggled to swallow it all.

Just as I thought I couldn't take anymore, Hunter used his hand in my hair to pull me up, being mindful of my sore foot. He gripped behind my thighs and lifted me up, my legs wrapping around his waist. I threw my arms around his neck. Our mouths collided, his tongue seeking access immediately.

Hunter walked forward and kneeled on the bed, shuffling our bodies up the sheets. I was lost in his taste and barely felt my curves being hugged by the mattress as he laid me down.

Running his hands down to my knees, he brought them up to rest on his shoulders as he settled between my legs. I looked down at him through hooded eyes. He was a fucking specimen of a man.

He met my gaze and licked his lips. "Your turn, baby."

The setting sun cast its warm, golden glow across the apartment. Hunter seemed to be growing antsy. His leg was bouncing furiously between us as we lay snuggled on the couch.

After Hunter made sure I was appropriately taken care of, he carried me to the shower. He held me to him and never let me lift a finger. As he washed my hair and ran a soapy washcloth over my skin, he whispered in my ear how amazing I was and how lucky he was.

But I was the lucky one.

Hunter took care of me more than anyone had in my entire life. Every time he looked at me, my heart skipped a beat and I found it hard to breathe. I never wanted this weekend to come to an end.

My foot nearly healed overnight, but Hunter never brought up wanting me to leave. Honestly, I didn't think I could go back to my empty apartment anyway.

Once we finished in the shower, Hunter ordered dinner and we sat on the couch to eat it. It was hands down the best cheeseburger I had ever eaten. It wasn't the typical one I have from the diner. It was somehow so much better.

After we ate, he cleaned everything up while making sure I never left the couch, then he put on a movie. I wasn't sure where the time had gone. It seemed the hours simply flew by wrapped up in Hunter's arms.

As I laid there with my head tucked against his chest, it felt like Hunter wanted to tell me something but was holding back. It worried me. I wanted to ask but I also didn't want to pop the bubble that had surrounded us.

What if he's trying to figure out how to kick me out?

No. He would have said something if that was it. But then, what would he be hiding?

The back of my throat started to burn as my brain convinced me that Hunter was just being nice. He didn't really care about me. The last forty-eight hours meant nothing to him

Deep down, I knew these thoughts were irrational but I couldn't stop them. Unshed tears gathered in the corners of my eyes, making it hard to focus on the television. I brought my hand up to wipe them away and took a shaky breath.

"Hey," Hunter whispered, kissing the top of my head. "You okay, sweetheart?

I nodded my head. He tightened his grip on me as he ran his hand up and down my arm. My chest tightened at his caring gesture, causing tears to slip down my cheeks. A small sob escaped my throat when I tried to exhale.

Hunter pulled me into his lap, his strong arms pressing me against him. The dam of emotions broke open. He held me as I cried.

What felt like hours was probably only minutes. Hunter ran his hand up and down my spine, a comforting motion that had me sinking into his embrace. When the tears dried, he didn't try to force me to talk right away. We simply sat there in silence.

I pulled away and his hand remained on my lower back. When I met his gaze, I expected to see disgust or even anger. Instead, his eyes held their own sadness and the corners of his lips were turned down. His thumb came up to brush away a stray tear, cupping my cheek when he finished.

The gesture calmed my nerves, silencing my racing mind. Even though I had just been convinced that Hunter hated me a few minutes ago. All this sex was screwing with my mind

"Sweetheart, if you want to talk about it, I'm here. But no pressure." He kissed my forehead then sat back, dropping his hand and putting space between us. I wanted to pull him to me and drown in his warmth. His golden eyes stared directly into me, lighting me on fire from the inside.

"I was convinced you wanted me to leave and were trying to figure out a nice way to kick me out." I forced a pitiful laugh, hoping it helped to hide some of my insecurities. "I mean, it's okay if you do... I won't hold it against you." I stared at my hands in my lap, unsure what to do with them.

"I don't want you to leave."

"Okay, I–" I went to stand, but my head snapped up as I processed his words. "You *don't* want me to leave?"

"Nope. Not right now. Not tomorrow." He put his hand on top of mine. "Not ever, if I'm being completely honest."

"Wait, what?"

"I want you to stay. For as long as you want. You don't have to leave."

I crashed my lips to his, forcing my tongue past his teeth as I deepened the kiss. Hunter gripped my hips and pulled me to him. I moved to straddle his legs as fingers roamed up my side, sliding over my skin. His touch reignited the fire inside me, an irresistible pressure growing between my legs. His hardening cock pressed into me from below as my hands slid under the hem of his shirt.

"Wait," I panted, pushing off his chest. Hunter's thumbs brushed the underside of my breasts and I had to force myself to focus. "You were all antsy. That's why I was worried."

"I don't want to talk about that right now." He pushed his hips up, the friction of our pants on my clit sending electricity up my spine. My nipples pebbled as he brushed his thumbs over them. He kissed along my jaw, marking a path with his lips to the sensitive spot behind my ear.

"Okay," I muttered, lost in the pleasure he was offering me. My hands wrapped around his neck as I fought to stay upright. "If you change your mind…"

"I won't. The only thing I want to hear right now is my name coming from those perfect lips of yours while you grind on my cock. Understood?" He grazed his teeth along my skin, sending a new wave of pleasure through me.

"Yes, sir," I moaned, digging my nails into his skin.

"Good fucking girl."

Chapter Nine

Hunter

Saturday Night

The full moon hung high in the sky. Standing at the open window in my bedroom, I watched as ominous clouds rolled over it. My skin was crawling, an itch I couldn't scratch away. My wolf growled in the back of my mind and demanded to hunt. If I left now, I could still fulfill the need gnawing at my stomach.

But what if I didn't?

There was never any guarantee that the first kill would suffice. There were countless hunting trips where I remained shifted for days.

No, I refused to let Rachael think I left her for even a second. She had worked herself up to the verge of a panic attack simply from the thought that I was going to kick her out.

Why hadn't I told her what the real issue was?

I should have been completely honest with her from the beginning, but I had been too scared. Rachael was more important to me than any witch's curse could ever be. I couldn't lose her.

I didn't know how I was going to make this work but I would. Maybe I could tell my friends. Benny alone connected with more magical beings in this town in the last few months than in the years I had lived here. He was bound to know someone who could help. Or I could chat with Azalea tomorrow when she and Theo got home from their trip.

Bottom line, something could be done.

Right?

I stalked back to the bed, slipped off my t-shirt, and slid in next to Rachael. My skin felt like it was on fire but all I wanted to do was hold Rachael.

Earlier, she had found her release on my lap and proceeded to pass out only a few minutes later on my shoulder. I had simply held onto her, relishing in the way her body fit so perfectly against mine.

When the sun had fully set and the living room was blanketed in darkness, I carried Rachael to bed and tucked her in. She hadn't moved since, her chest rising and falling steadily. I brushed a loose curl out of her face. She was so peaceful when she slept, her features void of burdensome emotions that constantly plagued her.

I would do whatever it took to make sure she stayed happy and safe.

This woman was it for me.

I loved her.

The wind blew through my fur as I tracked her scent. It hung in the air around me, marking a path through the trees. The full moon above me lit my way. My paws dug into the soft ground and kicked up dirt with each stride. Leaves crackled and sticks snapped ahead of me. She wasn't trying to hide her steps, running away on pure adrenaline.

I would catch her.

Use her.

Breed her.

Those were the only thoughts running through my mind.

She had stopped, crouched behind some brush. Space between the branches gave me just enough open space to see her. She tried to catch her breath, the hand on her chest rising and falling rapidly gave indication to such. The hunt was over too soon, but I had my prize either way.

I rounded the brush and branches scraped against my back as I stalked towards her. She scrambled backwards, her palms sliding along the dirt as she tried to stand. A low growl from deep inside me made her freeze and then I pounced.

My front legs pinned her arms against her side. "Hunter?" *she gasped but her voice sounded far away.*

It didn't matter.

I shoved my nose between her legs, loving that she was already soaking wet for me. My tongue lapped out to taste her and I was transported to my own personal paradise.

Use her.

Breed her.

I moved up her body and ran my tongue along her skin as she trembled beneath me.

When my body was fully on top of hers, I caught her gaze. The moonlight allowed me to make out her gorgeous features. Sweat lined her brow from the chase. Her heart was pounding in her chest. I could see her pulse through the vein in her neck. I ran my tongue along it, tasting her arousal mixed with fear.

Fear...

"Hunter," she moaned. "Please. Don't tease me." *Her begging went straight to my cock. There was no doubt she wanted this, me buried deep in her warm pussy.*

I slid along her folds to coat myself in her arousal. She bucked her hips as my head rubbed against her clit. The tip of my cock easily found her entrance from there. I slipped inside her, eliciting another loud moan.

Breed her.

I pumped hard and fast, my knot pulsing as it urged me on. But it wasn't enough. I craved more. The taste of copper flooded my mouth as my teeth sank into her flesh. Pain and pleasure, exactly what she needed.

"Hunter!" she screamed, but not from pleasure. The sound reverberated through my skull. I blinked and slowly, the trees around me dissolved. It was all just a dream…

No. A nightmare.

Because Rachael was actually under me, her arms pinned against her side and my cock buried between her legs. It wasn't paws holding her down though. My fingers dug into her skin as blood ran down her neck from several teeth marks that marred her beautiful skin.

I scrambled backwards, nearly falling off the edge of the bed and onto my ass as my legs tangled in my pants. My hands shook. My stomach was in knots and last night's dinner threatened to make a return. Rachael's fingers brushed across her neck, pulling away quickly when she made contact with the wound. Crimson liquid clung to her hand.

"Rachael, I–" I shifted forward, wanting to check on her, to take care of her. She flinched away from me and I stopped. When her gaze finally met mine, her eyes were wide with fear. My stomach dropped. My chest tightened. The one thing that I never wanted to happen finally did.

She was scared. Of me.

"Sweetheart, please," I whispered while reaching out my hand, like I was trying to coax a wounded animal towards me. "I am so sorry."

Her eyes flickered between my outstretched arm and my face. It was clear that she was fighting that internal battle. The fight or flight. Her body was visibly shaking as it tried to figure out what to do. Tears fell down her face and all I wanted to do was wipe them away.

I should have grabbed her, clung to her and made her listen. Explained it all to her.

But I broke her trust.

So when she ran, I didn't stop her.

I listened as her bare feet slapped against my floor and the door slammed shut. The sound vibrated against the walls, shattering my heart in the process. This was all my fault and I didn't know if I would be able to fix it.

CHAPTER TEN
Rachael

Sunday Morning

My bed was cold. I had grown too accustomed to Hunter's heat and no amount of blankets had the same effect. Sunlight filtered through my blinds, warming my skin but the chill I felt was deep in my bones.

I laid on my side, facing the window, and my hand rested on my neck where I had covered the bite mark with a large bandage. Sleep never came last night.

When Hunter had climbed on top of me, I had barely been awake. He was panting heavily as if he had just run a marathon. I remembered the way his eyes practically glowed above me, but it was as if he was looking straight through me. All rational thought left my body when he marked a path along my neck with his tongue. Hunter had known how to play my body like a fiddle.

I knew something was wrong though when I moaned his name and he didn't respond. He enjoyed making me squirm underneath him with his dirty praise. The man who had been above me was not Hunter, the man I had started falling in love with.

Worry had coursed through my veins when he had pushed inside of me bare. I could feel his knot at my entrance and it scared me. We had been using condoms all weekend and never had the conversation otherwise. I wasn't on birth control and who knew if that scumbag ex of mine gave me anything.

I had been lost in thought and didn't notice Hunter's bared teeth until it was too late. The pain that ripped through my body had been unbearable. Horrified, I had watched Hunter blink down at me in confusion then all of a sudden it was like he woke up.

He had tried to comfort me, but I couldn't let him. He had promised to never hurt me, told me he cared for me. The thought of him touching me after what he had done sent my mind spiraling into a panic attack.

So I ran.

My apartment had been unlocked but everything was in pristine order. Hunter had said Benny was going to fix it up and replace the locks. He must have cleaned up, too. There was no trace of that night. I had made a mental note to track down Benny and ask him about new keys. Marching to my room, I had crawled under my sheets and cried, sobs wrecking my body well until the first rays of morning sun peeked into the room.

Now, here I was.

I was still wearing Hunter's shirt. Tucking my nose into the collar, I breathed in his scent. Pine and oak. Like walking through a forest after a summer rain.

Even though he had hurt me, I didn't want this to be over. Something told me there was more to the story. I knew I was crazy to even be considering it, or maybe it had been all the mindblowing orgasms. Maybe I could hear Hunter out and listen to his side of things.

Absolutely not. You were not jumping out of the frying pan and into the fire.

But Chad had been horrible. He had no respect for me. It had been all about him and what he wanted. I had just been too scared to leave him and start something new, but it was easy when he stopped respecting my boundaries. Why was I comparing him to Hunter?

Rolling onto my back, I stared at my ceiling. It was official. This was the last time I was letting my vagina make decisions. She was a horrible influence. I grabbed a pillow and threw it over my face, screaming out my frustrations. *How did I find myself in the middle of this mess?*

A tiny meow broke through the deprecating self-reflection. I sat up and saw a tiny black cat sitting on the edge of my bed.

"Thor?" I asked. He meowed in response and padded across my blanket towards me. When he reached my legs, I crossed them under me as he sat.

He meowed again, but this one was longer. It felt like he was asking me something.

"Shit hit the fan, Thor. I'm not sure what I'm supposed to do." I reached out, running my fingers through his short black hair. "And now I'm talking to a cat as if he'll respond."

He came closer and settled in my lap. I continued petting him, his purrs of contentment filling the silence in the room. It was actually very relaxing. We sat there together and, with each passing second, I could feel the anxiety leaving my body. The anger and regret coursing through me minutes ago dissipated.

A knock echoing through my apartment broke me out of my trance. Thor stretched as he left my lap, then strutted out of my room. Grabbing a pair of pajama shorts, I jumped into them as I followed him to the small entryway.

He sat in front of the door and looked up at it as if waiting for me to open it. Peeking through the peephole, I recognized the red curls from the night in Hunter's living room. I barely had the door unlocked and open when the short, stocky man burst into my apartment and started berating his cat.

"Thor Loki Fee, what are you doing up here?"

I chuckled at the fact this cat had a full name. Benny shot me a quick look before returning his attention to his cat. I closed the door behind the two of them, leaving them alone in my entryway while I walked to my kitchen. Coffee would be a necessity if I was going to keep up with this man

"You know I could care less if you wander the halls on the first floor but you can't go breaking into apartments up here. You're going to get shipped off to the animal shelter!" Thor meowed in response. Benny didn't stop, the two of them going at it for several minutes while my pot of coffee brewed. I tried my best not to laugh at the crazy scene taking place in my living room.

Is it any crazier than when Hunter was a wolf and lying unconscious on your floor?

Touché, brain.

I sipped my coffee, letting the warmth flow through my body and chase away the chill that had settled. My stomach rumbled and I thought about those waffles Hunter had made. They were easily the best tasting thing I had ever eaten.

The things that followed were pretty great too. I had never felt so empowered in the bedroom. Hunter did more for my confidence in one weekend than I had been able to do in the last few years.

Hunter...

Benny came up beside me, pulling me from my thoughts. Thor was perched on his shoulders. "I'm Benny. Nice to officially meet you." He held out his hand and I shook it, holding back the laugh at the sudden professionalism. Like I didn't just watch him talking to his cat for the last five minutes.

"I'm so sorry about him." Benny gestured to Thor with his head.

"No apology needed." I chuckled, reminding myself what Thor had walked in on. "I think he knew I needed the company."

"He told me he likes the sun spot on your bed. So it seems his motivation for finding his way into your apartment was purely selfish."

"That's okay." I reached out to scratch under Thor's chin. He sank into my touch, his neck stretching out as he closed his eyes. I spoke directly to Thor, "You can come lay in my bed whenever you want."

"Especially if you're going to be spending more time downstairs." Benny crossed his arms and leaned his hip against the counter.

I nearly choked on the gulp of coffee in my mouth once my brain caught up. "What do you mean?" I sputtered out between coughs.

"In all the time I've known Hunter, he has never had interest in a woman. Especially not a human one. No offense."

"None taken, I guess."

"He didn't say it, that night he brought you down to his place, but Liliana and I both knew. Hunter is absolutely smitten with you."

"Who says smitten these days?"

"Well, I do. And it's true. Plus, Thor told me what he walked in on the other day. You and Hunter in his bedroom." Thor meowed from Benny's shoulder then jumped down. He rubbed between my legs as if apologizing for telling on us.

"It's okay, buddy." I bent down and scratched between his ears. He meowed approvingly once more then meandered out of the kitchen, towards my room.

I turned my attention back to Benny.

"So why are you up here instead of down there with him?" he asked while grabbing a mug from my cabinet and pouring himself a cup of coffee.

"It's a long story," I muttered. Benny wasn't my friend, he was Hunter's. There was no way he wanted to listen to me. Worse yet, he would take Hunter's side and tell me how dramatic I was being.

"Just because I'm his friend, doesn't mean I'm not aware of his shortcomings," Benny said, as if responding to my thoughts.

"How did you–"

"Doesn't matter," he interrupted, waving off my confusion. "If anything, Hunter being my friend probably makes me the most qualified to listen. I know that man can get inside his own head sometimes." He walked over to the small table I had set up in the kitchen corner, coffee mug in hand.

He gestured to the empty seat next to him. "Time to spill, darling."

Chapter Eleven

Hunter

Sunday Night

A heavy weight laid across my chest. Guilt wrecked my body. I laid on the floor in my living room, unsure what else to do. Staring at the ceiling, I wanted to barge into Rachael's apartment and apologize.

But that would be pointless.

So I distracted myself. The day went by too slowly. Her smell was everywhere and all I could do was fight off the memories of our time together. They seeped in through the cracks. Even sleep evaded me. Every time I closed my eyes, her scream echoed in my ears.

I had hurt her.

The one person who I had come to love. It may be crazy saying that after only one weekend with her but something inside me knew. Rachael was my forever.

And I fucking screwed it up.

My wolf screamed at me to leave and I wanted to. It would be better for everyone if I disappeared into the woods, shifted, and let the curse take its course. If I had hurt Rachael in my sleep, the only person I truly ever cared for, there was no telling what else could happen as my impulse control dwindled.

"Damn it!" I groaned into the empty space, throwing my arm over my eyes.

A meow echoed my curse. I sat straight up as a flash of black fur preceded the sharp prick of claws dragging through my bare skin.

"What the fucking hell?" I looked around for the offending bastard and found Thor perched on the arm of my chair. "Seriously?"

It would seem the weight I had been feeling was, in fact, real and not just my overbearing anxiety trying to suffocate me.

I stood from the floor and made my way over to the cat. Thor seemed unphased by my approach, casually cleaning his paw.

He hissed as I scooped him up. "You seriously need to stop coming in here, you little asshole." I dangled him out in front of me, keeping his tiny weapons away from my bare skin. The scratch on my chest stung as the open air made contact.

Thor was meowing but I refused to open my mind and chat with him. This little fucker needed to stop breaking in to my apartment. I opened my front door, ready to throw Thor out, when I noticed Benny standing there posed to knock.

"Hey, Hunter," he said. "Have you seen– THOR, WE TALKED ABOUT THIS!"

Benny grabbed his cat from my arms, sat Thor down at his feet, then pointed down the hall. "Go home. Before I drop you off at an animal shelter myself."

Thor walked away, his tail swishing behind him until he disappeared.

Benny turned to me, pointing his finger towards my chest. "Your turn."

"Not right now, Benny." I tried to close the door but he stopped it.

"Oh no you don't." He stepped into my apartment, letting the door shut behind him. "I've got a bone to pick with you, too. You hurt Rachael."

"It wasn't intentional, Benny!" I yelled and spun to face him. My wolf scratched at the edges of my mind. "It was the full moon and I thought I was just dreaming but it turned out– Wait, you talked to Rachael?"

"Yeah." He folded his arms over his chest and glared at me. I closed the distance between us in one large stride, grabbing his shoulders.

"Is she okay? Is she hurt? Do we need to get Liliana?" Concern flooded my body. I shouldn't have just let her run away without checking on her.

"Physically she's fine." He shrugged me off. Sidestepping me, he walked to the kitchen and rummaged through my fridge. I stared at his back, waiting for him to give me more.

"You got anything good to eat?" he asked over his shoulder.

"Are you kidding me, Benny?" He turned, closing the fridge door. There was a glass bottle of something in his hand and he popped the lid off of it.

"You broke her heart, man." He took a drink then glared at me.

"I know." My shoulders fell.

"So what are you gonna do about it?"

"What do you mean?"

"How are you going to fix that?" He gestured to the ceiling with the bottle in his hand.

"I don't think I can." I shook my head. There was no fixing this. Rachael would be crazy for even considering forgiving me. I didn't deserve it.

"Never say never."

"I can't be who she needs me to be. Not now."

"Does this have something to do with your hunting trips?" He tipped the rest of the liquid from the bottle into his mouth.

"Maybe."

"I had a feeling there was always more to them. But who was I to push you?"

"I should have told you and Liliana sooner."

"Well, you can tell me now."

Rubbing my hand down my face, I took a deep breath then walked to the kitchen. I searched the cabinets for the bottle of whiskey I kept around for the rare occasions I craved a drink. Finally finding it, I filled a random mug halfway with the amber colored liquid.

Then the truth came out. I told Benny about my great grandpa and the witch's curse. Pacing the kitchen floor, I spilled my guts about how I felt for Rachael and how stupid I was for putting her in danger. When I finished, I refused to meet Benny's eyes. They would hold judgment and I couldn't handle that.

"Hunter," Benny whispered, "will you stop pacing, please?" I froze and gripped the edge of the counter.

"Let me see if I understand this." He came up beside me, leaning against his back. "Your family lineage was cursed to hunt during the full moon. And if you don't, the next time you shift, you're stuck as a wolf? That's kind of screwed up."

"That's the gist of it." I pinched the bridge of my nose. "Fucking hell, this is all sorts of messed up."

"You can say that again." A dull thud rang through my skull as Benny's hand smacked the back of it.

"What was that for?" I rubbed the spot, not that it hurt any worse than Rachael hitting me with her bat.

"You definitely should have told me and Liliana sooner. We could have helped you, figured something out!"

"I've never felt this defeated, Benny. It feels like my heart has been ripped out of my chest. My wolf is telling me to leave and I might listen. Because I'm not sure there is anything left for me here." I clutched the counter, my knuckles turning white.

"Hunter..." His hand on my shoulder was barely noticeable as anger coursed through me. My muscles tightened and the cracking of laminate filled the kitchen. Particleboard crumbled around my feet.

I could hear Benny speaking but couldn't make out what he was saying over the haze settling in my mind. My impulse control dwindled as the animal instincts started to take over. This was it...

But then, a scream rang through my ears. One that was far too familiar, but not in the way my mind remembered.

"Hunter!"

I stood up straight, turning to Benny. His brows were raised in question at my sudden change. He hadn't heard what I did. *Shit.*

"What's going on?" Benny yelled behind me as I ran from my apartment, not bothering to explain to him the fear coursing through me.

Rachael was in trouble.

CHAPTER TWELVE
Rachael

A knock at the door caused me to jump, nearly dropping the plate I had been carrying. I wasn't expecting Benny back until tomorrow. After our heart to heart, he had given me the new keys to my apartment then went to grab Thor to take him home. He told me he would come by tomorrow around dinner time, to once again fetch Thor who would no doubt be lounging in that sun spot and keeping me company.

I put the dish in my dishwasher then headed to the door. *Maybe Hunter had come to apologize. Would I listen to what he had to say?*

Lost in thought, I didn't look through the peephole and when I saw it wasn't Hunter, my breath caught in my lungs.

Chad stalked through the living room towards me as I slowly backed into the kitchen. A gun hung loosely in his palm. His eyes were wild, like an animal, staring me down like a predator hunting its prey.

My heart beat wildly in my chest but I did my best to control my breathing. I couldn't show Chad I was scared. I couldn't show weakness. He would latch onto it and use it against me.

"Chad, honey, why don't you sit down? I can make you some dinner."

He continued his path towards me as I pressed myself into the counter. The menacing smile that spread across his face sent a shiver down my spine.

"I'm definitely hungry, little lady." He towered over me now, shoving his nose into my neck. I could smell the cheap alcohol on his breath. My stomach turned and I swallowed the bile that rose up the back of my throat.

I tried to turn my head away, but his rough hand grabbed my jaw, yanking my face towards him. "No, you don't. You're going to look at me, and you're going to thank me for coming back for you."

I tried to shake my head, but Chad held it still. He ran his nose along my jaw. His mouth was on top of my ear.

"That asshole with roid rage who thought he was saving you last time won't be interrupting us this go around. I've been waiting. I know he's left you on your own." His hand on my jaw went to my throat, using it as a point of leverage.

My lungs stopped working and my chest tightened as I tried to draw in a breath. Tears burned the back of my eyes. He pressed his body into mine as he spoke, "Now, we're going to have a little bit of fun."

There was only one thought that ran through my head.

"Hunter!"

But it wasn't just a thought. It was a scream. One that was backed by every fiber of my being. Because I knew he would come, even if he thought I was upset with him. Even if I wasn't sure what our future held.

Hunter would come.

As expected, Chad attempted to silence me. He slapped his large hand over my mouth. While it muffled my voice, I refused to stop. I took in as much air as I could to try again.

Pain ripped through my skull as Chad brought the butt of the gun down to the side of my head. His motions were sloppy but it was enough to silence me.

"You stupid fucking bitch." I could barely hear Chad over the ringing in my ears. Darkness invaded my vision, making everything incredible blurry. My chest expanded rapidly as pure panic set in.

It felt like minutes had passed, even hours. *Where was Hunter?*

As if on cue, the familiar sound of splintering wood broke through the chaos surrounding me. I could just make out Hunter's silhouette as I blinked, helping my vision to slowly clear.

"Get your fucking hands off of her." His tone was deadly, even more so than the last time he said those words.

Chad spun around and took me with him. His arm gripped across my shoulder, pressing my back against his sweaty chest.

"Tell him to leave us alone, sweetness. We don't need him, do we?" he whispered into my ear. My head was swimming and I tried to focus on the man in front of me.

Chad used the forgotten gun to caress my cheek, sending sparks of panic down my spine. "Tell him," he snarled.

My body shook and I fought to stay upright, clawing at Chad's arm. I couldn't stop the tears that fell down my cheeks as I swallowed hard. "Hunter, help..."

That was all I could get out when cold metal pressed against the side of my head. My blood ran cold. I clamped my mouth shut to keep from losing my dinner.

"Last chance," he threatened. The tip of the gun pinched my skin as Chad pushed it further into my temple. My lungs seized, unable to push air out or bring it in.

Hunter's body shook wildly as he watched us. His hands balled into fists at his side. His features tightened, morphing into something more.

Rage.

The dark hair on his arms thickened, spreading along his body as his clothes melted away.

Hunter was no longer human. The only familiar part of the wolf in front of us was the glowing golden eyes. Chad's hold on me tightened as he pointed the gun towards him.

"D–don't come any cl–closer." Chad's voice wavered as the hand holding the gun shook. A prickling sensation took over my hands and feet. Hunter stalked towards us, teeth bared.

"I mean it." Chad sounded more confident this time as he pressed the gun against my head once more. A whimper escaped through my clenched teeth. "Come closer and I'll blow her brains out. I don't give a fuck if this bitch lives or dies."

A flash of fur rushed towards us as I closed my eyes.

A scream tore from my throat as the gun went off.

I crumpled to the ground, no longer held hostage against Chad's body. My ears rang from the gunshot. Slowly, I opened my eyes. The ringing was replaced by Chad's screams as Hunter clamped down on the wrist that had held a gun only seconds ago. It was now laying useless next to his fingers.

The sound of crunching bone bounced around my skull while Chad's screams suddenly cut off. There was blood everywhere, a pool of it gathering under his severed hand. Chad laid motionless as Hunter moved on to gnawing at his forearm. I sat up and stared at the scene, unable to move or speak.

"What's going on? I heard a gunshot." I recognized Benny's voice. "Who the fuck broke this door ag–Oh no."

"Rachael." His footsteps vibrated the floor as he came up behind me. I was too transfixed on the scene unfolding in front of me. He placed a hand on my shoulder. "We need to go. The cops will be here soon."

"No." I shook my head, refusing to look away. Hunter sank his teeth into Chad's neck. "Not without him."

"Honey, it's not safe. He's not changing back. He can't."

"Wh—what do you mean?"

As if hearing us talk about him, Hunter turned his head. His golden eyes were wide in a familiar way. This was how he looked last night.

Did that mean his wolf was in control? Why was Benny saying he couldn't change back? Was this the curse?

Too many questions bounced around in my head and they went unanswered as the wolf took a step towards us. Benny yanked at my arm, trying to get me to move. My body refused to budge. My eyes were locked with Hunter's.

"Hunter," I begged. "Please. Come back."

He took another step towards me, then collapsed on his side. A patch of blood-soaked fur covered his abdomen.

"Hunter!" I screamed, rushing forward.

He whimpered as I pressed my hands into his side.

"I'm going to go get Liliana," Benny said, running from my apartment. "And try to buy us some time with the cops!"

I paid him no mind as I watched Hunter's chest rise and fall rapidly. Pressing harder, I willed the blood back into his body. This couldn't be the end.

Time slowed. I met his gaze, his eyes softening. Tears ran down my cheeks.

Everything I wanted to say to him stuck in my throat. I wanted him to know I forgave him, that none of this was his fault. I wanted him to know how much he meant to me.

I wanted to tell him...

"I love you, Hunter," I whispered, just as his eyes fluttered closed.

Liliana rushed into my apartment. Her gasp echoed in the now silent space. She rushed forward, placing her hands along his body. I laid my head on Hunter's chest and willed it to move.

"Rachael..." Liliana's voice was soft as she placed her hand on my shoulder. "He's gone."

"I'm not leaving him." I pressed my cheek further into his fur. It was still warm and soft.

"It's okay. I'm going to go find Benny." Her hand fell away as her feet shuffled along my floor. My front door squeaked, signaling their departure. I silently thanked them for giving me space.

How had I fucked this up so royally?

My body trembled with the need to scream but I couldn't muster the energy. I knew I was in shock, trying to process Hunter actually being gone. The longer I laid there, the harder it became to get up. My body was numb and I was certain my mind was playing tricks on me when I felt a hand on my back. It was too familiar.

"Rachael..." Hunter's voice mixed with the fog in my head. I pressed my cheek further into Hunter's chest, wanting to be as close to him as possible, but became confused when it no longer felt like fur.

I bolted upright, staring down in disbelief at a naked Hunter on my floor. He sat up and wrapped his arms around me. I climbed into his lap and sobbed into his neck.

"It's okay, sweetheart," he soothed, his hand rubbing my back as the other kept me firmly against him. "I'm so sorry."

I shook my head. "I'm sorry. If I had stayed and listened, I wouldn't have been in this situation and you wouldn't have had to come rescue me for a second time."

"There is no way I'm letting you take even an ounce of blame for this. I should have told you everything. I was scared of losing you and that's exactly what happened." I sat back in his arms, meeting his gaze. His eyes were filled with sadness and it shattered my heart.

"I told you I wouldn't leave." My voice broke on the last word, thinking about how much he must have hated when I ran away. His hands cupped my cheeks.

"You had every right. I put you in danger. I hurt you. It should have never come to that. I feel like all I have are empty promises." He dropped his hands, grabbing mine and bringing them to his lips.

His thumbs brushed over my knuckles as he laid my palms against his chest. Warmth spread through my body.

"I love you, Rachael. I don't expect you to say it back. But if you let me, I will spend every day trying to prove it to you. You deserve more than I can give you but I will never stop giving you everything I've got."

I pulled his face to mine, claiming his mouth with a kiss that quickly left me breathless. I broke our kiss and rested my forehead against his. My hands searched his abdomen, certain my fingers would find evidence of a gunshot wound.

"Rachael," he whispered. His hands wrapped around mine and brought them back up to his chest.

"I just– There's no– I was–" I couldn't form a complete sentence.

"I'm okay." He pulled away, planting kisses on my palms. "Does this mean you forgive me?"

"Of course, Hunter. I forgave you the second you came bursting through my door a second time." Our lips met once more. "And I love you, too. It might be crazy but something about this feels right. Like I'm where the universe wants me to be."

Hunter picked me up with his hands on my hips, spinning me around my living room. I couldn't help the giggle that bubbled to the surface.

"Rachael, honey? We're going to have to move Hunt–Oh my gods!" Benny yelled from behind us. Hunter put me down on my feet and we both turned to look towards the door. Benny and Liliana were standing just inside the doorway, both with huge smiles on their faces.

"Hunter, clothes!" Liliana exclaimed while throwing her hands over her eyes.

I turned to Hunter, having completely forgotten his state of undress during our confessions. "I always meant to ask you that. Where do your clothes go when you shift?"

Hunter looked down at me, his eyebrow raised. "You know, I have no clue." He looked over to Benny and Liliana, who still had her eyes covered. We exchanged glances before we all burst out laughing.

EPILOGUE

Hunter

One Week Later

"Hunter, did you finish up the apple crumble for dinner?" Rachael called to me from the bathroom.

"I'm finishing it now, sweetheart!" I put the last touch on the dish then headed to the fridge for the chilled bottle of wine.

We rescheduled the dinner from last week, seeing as I shifted and caused issues. Specifically, gnawing off Chad's hand.

Benny used his connections in town to help cover up the incident. The cops hadn't looked too closely at our story about the gunshot being a blank once we produced a limbless Chad. We convinced them that he had wandered into the woods drunk and when we found him, his hand was missing. They chalked it up to some sort of coyote attack. An ambulance took him to a trauma hospital a few towns over. The last we heard, Chad had been too terrified to talk about the incident.

After I had put on some clothes, I convinced Rachael to let Liliana give her a once over. I hated to even think about Chad's hands on my woman. Theo and Azalea had stopped by during it all, curious as to where everyone was. With everyone gathered in one place, it was easy to spill my secrets to them all.

Azalea used her magic to search for the origin of the spell and found faint traces of what she referred to as the True Love's Curse. Apparently, the witch who hexed my great grandpa had doomed my family line to the effects of the curse until one of us sacrificed ourselves for our fated mate. It was strange, thinking that something I never would have thought twice of doing was the thing to break the curse.

After gathering her necessities, Rachael had come back to my apartment. She had spent every night since with me. Tonight, I would make sure she knew I never wanted her to leave. The whole fated mates thing would hopefully help seal the deal.

Soft hands wrapped around my waist, slipping under my shirt. Rachael pressed herself against my back. Even through my shirt, I felt her warm breath against my skin. Her heart beat in rhythm with my own.

I turned in her arms, pulling her against me and pressing my nose into her hair. Every day, I thanked whoever was listening for giving me this woman.

She leaned back, looking up at me with those beautiful eyes. "Are you ready to go, love?"

"Not quite yet." I pressed my lips to hers, drinking her in and cherishing every moment. She melted in my arms. I held her to me, deepening our kiss.

When we both pulled away, our gazes held each other as we stood there breathless. I tucked a few loose strands of hair behind her ear. My fingers lingered on her cheeks.

"I love you," I whispered, smiling down at her.

"I love you, too." She ran her hand through my beard and cupped my jaw. "Now we better leave. Or Benny will come knocking. He's still pissed about having to fix my apartment door for a second time."

I laughed. She was right, of course. Thor would probably come sneaking in to report back to Benny if we weren't there soon.

Grabbing the dessert in one hand and Rachael's hand in my other, I led us out of my apartment down the hall to Benny's place. We stood at the door, but before I knocked, I bent down and stole one more kiss.

"Let's get this over with," I said. "So I can take you back home and worship you the way you deserve."

She winked at me as the door opened in front of us. Benny welcomed us both and ushered us towards the open living room where all of our friends had congregated.

Rachael pressed into my side, her arm snaking around my waist. I held her against me as her body shaped to mine. Standing in this room and looking at everyone, I realized just how happy I had become. Something I never thought would be possible.

And to think, none of this would have happened if it weren't for me being the wolf next door.

NOTE FROM AUTHOR

Dear Reader,

Thank you for reading! If you enjoyed your time with Hunter and Rachael, or even if you didn't, please consider leaving a review. Many readers do not understand just how important ratings and reviews are to self-published authors, especially on sites like Amazon. Even just a few words do more good than you will ever know. It helps push our books to new potential readers.

So, thank you in advance for all your help! Without you, I would not be able to write and share my stories.

xoxo,

Delaine

ACKNOWLEDGEMENTS

Number two is in the books. Wow, just wow. My debut novel was written as a way to process a lot of trauma. This book was written because of a fun little idea I had. Actually, it started as a short story that I had planned to submit to an anthology. But as I started writing, these characters had more to tell me. By that I mean they wanted lots of spice and care scenes. So I kept writing and decided these two deserved a novella. Now, onto the must deserved special thanks!

To my favorite queen Jessica, this is your love letter. There is no exaggeration when I say I could not have done this without you. Seriously. You were my sounding board for this one and I'm not sure I would have finished it if you weren't encouraging me every step of the way. I am so very grateful to have you in my life and I'm honored to call you a friend. Please know I'm here for it all and there is no getting rid of me. Also, don't forget to delete my Kindle history.

To Rianna, I love your face. Thank you for everything you've done for me. I can't believe how far our friendship has come since last year. It was so much fun creating this world with you and I hope we can do it again.

To the IRL Rachael, thank you for letting me use your name and seeing it as an honor. Truly, I'm the honored one and am so grateful to have your friendship in all the things.

To Lindsey, you didn't really get any of my unhinged thoughts during the writing of this one but it felt wrong not to include you back here. You're a dedicated supporter and one of my best friends. Thank you for the endless faith and I can't wait for you to read this one.

To Amilia and Kelsey, thank you for being kickass beta readers! Your enthusiasm for my story made me even more excited for the release.

To Amanda, thank you for taking my subpar concept design and creating the most beautiful cover. I am absolutely obsessed!

To Bree and my Australia girlies (you know who you are), Finding Gwen would not have been the success it was without you. I know you have my back no matter what and I hope you enjoyed this one just as much.

To the Cincy Author Coven, the support has been non-stop. I truly don't know if I would have survived this journey this far without you. It is important to find your community as a writer and I am lucky I found mine.

To my family, especially my late grandmother in law JoAnn, thank you for all your unconditional support. No matter how many "fucks" I use.

To all of my readers, thank you. Whether I know you personally or not, the fact you picked up my story and read it means the world to me. There will never be enough words to appropriately express my gratitude.

ABOUT THE AUTHOR

Delaine Walsh lives in Northern Kentucky with her husband and two fur babies. She enjoys writing emotional scenes with lots of spice.

When she's not home writing, she's scouring local bookstores for her next impulsive book purchase. Reading has always been an escape for her, and she hopes her stories provide that for others.